Sunset on Us

Houston Heights-Book 1

Gia Stone

Sunset on Us
Houston Heights- Book 1
Copyright © 2024 Gia Stone
All rights reserved.

ISBN: (ebook) 978-1-958136-87-4
(print) 978-1-964636-00-9

Inkspell Publishing
207 Moonglow Circle #101
Murrells Inlet, SC 29576

Edited By Yezanira Venecia
Cover art By Emily's World By Design

DEDICATION

TO ANYONE WHO FEELS BROKEN, THIS
SONG IS FOR YOU.

GIA STONE

CHAPTER ONE

Cheyenne Ford wrote songs for as long as she could remember. Before she knew how to write words, her songs were images that she scribbled in her tattered notebook. Once the alphabet had been introduced, her images became poems on paper, and melodies were played on her guitar. The guitar that she had saved up her allowance to buy. Nothing was given to her. Everything was earned, one way or another.

"Gotta Have My Man" was from her most recent album: *Truth, Shaken, Not Stirred.* Many questioned the title and whom the number one single was about it. Cheyenne Ford couldn't be bothered with these minor thoughts, and tonight was no different.

Gotta Have My Man
This song is for you, J

Button up
Tie me down
Screw it back on tight
Lid is sealed

I'm not healed but I'm moving on

It's a promise
For a purpose
I'm doing right
Taking a step

Give me one more chance
I just want to dance
I wanna dance with you

Gotta have my partner
Gotta have my man
Don't leave me standing all alone

Gotta have my partner
Gotta have my man
Don't leave me standing all alone

You were the last one to see my frown
You held me up
Saved by grace
You made this world a better place

I can't imagine you not around
Baby, I need you to stay in town
Give me one more chance
I just want to dance

Gotta have my partner
Gotta have my man
Don't leave me standing all alone

It was too soon to be back—back to the blue laws and the new gilded age with legislation and regulations that most thought were left half a century ago. Texas. Too many memories existed in this vast state. Definitely too many to deal with through the lens of sober eyes.

Cheyenne Ford was not one to miss a last call. Tonight would be no different. Time is a precarious thing. The pendulum can swing back and forth, but the sands drizzle through the neck the same for everyone.

"Dammit." Cheyenne's eyes shot glares at the clock. The nine was too early and the one meant she was too late. They missed the alcohol sales cutoff by one minute. Cheyenne should have skipped that last bathroom break. Surely, she could have held it for one more hour. Or at least fifteen minutes. That time was needed, but it was gone.

She glanced at Jamison. Not a crease on his forehead. His massive hands seemed relaxed as he gripped the steering wheel, not an ounce of stress. He was always so calm, even in moments of danger, which there had been several over the years. Jamison was like an old-fashioned glass of whiskey. His delivery was smooth and his charm was natural. That's why she loved him. Cheyenne was safe with him, always.

Jamison caught her eye like a lighthouse's beam. "Cheyenne, you can make it one night."

"I know I can, but I don't want to. You know it's difficult for me to be back here." Her lips formed into a perfect pout—one that was not practiced but rather wove into perfection around him.

Jamison's sea-green eyes left hers and returned to the road. "All right, princess, where to?"

Cheyenne tossed her head back as if her long ruby locks were able to shake off the tension of being back in this town. "The freaking Broken Spoke—take a right."

Jamison veered the Escalade into the gravel-filled path under the only light in the makeshift parking lot. He always parked under a light. Everything Jamison did was with intent and purpose. Cheyenne hopped out of the vehicle. Theirs was the only one without a gun rack or a GOP bumper sticker. Yes, indeed, she was back in Texas.

Cheyenne swallowed a huge gulp as fear filled her body. Even with Jamison at her side, this place was filled with trauma and remorse.

It was sixty degrees when they left Nashville this morning, but Cut and Shoot, Texas, was still hot at the end of October. The weather was like an addition to the heat that seared over Cheyenne's skin. A cool drink would help temper her thoughts and lose the heavy layers of armor. Cheyenne was sure of it. Peace had to be found, if only a shot's worth.

It had been eleven years since she left, and Cheyenne had never intended to return—even her parents had moved away—but this was something she had to do. It was the last sliver of a possibility. One of her favorite quotes was, "You have to make it matter to make it happen." And matter this did—more than all her awards, top 100 albums, and even herself. In moments of silence, when all she had were her thoughts, Cheyenne knew what mattered the most. Even if it meant going down a memory lane of pain.

Cheyenne skipped over to the other side of the car and swatted Jamison's muscular behind. He was like an industrialized walking machine. He put the Vin Diesels of the world to shame. And this was before he spoke a word. Once his heavy voice dropped a hello, it was over. He could get anyone to do anything for him, but part of his charm was that he didn't take advantage of it.

Jamison grabbed her hand. "Cheyenne, if you swat me, I'll swat you back." He lifted her over his head and carried her upside down over his shoulder into the bar, giving her a few swats on the way inside.

"Let me down," she fake pleaded through laughter. Jamison finally released her when they approached the bar and sat her ass onto a stool. It wasn't exactly red-carpet service, but it was an entrance. One that did not go unnoticed. Eyes were all on Cheyenne and the guy who delivered her back to the place patrons still considered her original home. Whispers began to make way through the darkened bar, accompanied by nods and smiles and even a few sneers—she wasn't liked by everyone.

Cheyenne took in the place. She had only been here a few times with a fake ID and a handful of giddiness. Everything had been so different then. Everything. But this place hadn't changed. It still looked the same: animal heads on the wall, sawdust on the floor, wagon wheels that held up plywood-varnished tables. Yes, this was the Broken Spoke. A place of broken hearts.

The bartender had his back turned as Jamison slid onto his stool. Cheyenne eyed the bartender. His shoulders were squared and the back of his bicep had a tattoo. A skull and maybe a frog? He turned around and took a step back as his eyes widened, almost as if he needed to regain his composure. "Hey there, Cheyenne, it's good to see you back."

Cheyenne swallowed. Was this Nick Jenkins? He seemed to have aged more than what Cheyenne had expected. If this was him. Possibly from the life behind the bar, or had he gone off to some military assignment? The military always seemed to come to the towns to recruit the next round of young adults with little to no options for a career. Enlistment through extinction of choices and lack of opportunity. It is a rarity to find a recruiting office in the more illustrious parts of town. But Cut and Shoot was far from illustrious or industrious. Mostly cattle and farmland folk. Cheyenne couldn't remember which part of town Nick clung to, but time had changed him. Whether it was the military or the darkened bar, either way, his blue eyes were not as bright as they once were.

"Hey, how are you?" This was a classic Cheyenne move: always pivot to the other person. Most people prefer to discuss themselves. Cheyenne was fine for someone else to have the mic. Despite being the star, Cheyenne always made everyone else in the room feel like they were the ones on stage. The one in the bright glow of the starlight. It was her best move for moments like this, and especially in a situation like tonight. It ended the Q and A for her and brought the focus onto the other person. Most of all, it would solve any queries about whether she recognized him.

Despite the detailed lyrics in her songs, she had tried to shut out the majority of her memories from Cut and Shoot. A quick scan of her limited social media gave her prompts of who married whom or what someone's nickname was. Nothing more than surface-level updates. She wished everything else about Cut and Shoot could be a white blank page. Even the quick peek at former classmates' posts gave a chill to other memories. The inner workings of her brain would freeze like an icicle in the sharpest formation. The tip was pointed, and it cut deep. Regardless of the avalanche that shifted inside, it was too hard to revisit. She did not want to participate in this reunion of faces from her past. Especially in this town. It wasn't as if she didn't care. If there was one solid thing about Cheyenne, it was that she cared about other people. Celebrityhood had never dug in too deep for her. Even designer jeans and fancy leather boots couldn't shake the sincerity in her heart.

Her painful melodies and heartfelt songs made her a fan favorite. The vulnerability with each lyric that bled into each tune. True happiness came from her guitar; the money was just the chocolate drizzle over the top. Being a celebrity meant being "on" no matter where you go. Impromptu meet and greets were part of the deal. Get recognized, get in character, and bring on that sweet Texas charm. Tonight might just be one of those types of situations. Cheyenne knew how to work the stage or room. On stage she could turn the mic over to the backup singers, and the crowd would go wild for the improv. A different verse never sung before, just for them. Fans loved it.

Cheyenne was sure this was Nick. Her smile was genuine and kind as she leaned in to hear him over the music. "You're doing well, then?"

"Good, real good. Gosh, you look amazing. Better than on the big screen. I've watched all your live performances."

Nick laughed. "How is that even possible? High school didn't seem that long ago, and then you took off so fast—"

"Hey, what do you have on tap?" Jamison interrupted him. He wouldn't let anyone entertain that discussion. Cheyenne couldn't have found a better person to shut it down. That discussion was not allowed, ever. Jamison knew this, and no one argued with Jamison.

"Oh, uh, we've got Saint Arnolds, Bud, No Label, and Miller." Nick motioned toward the draft lineup behind him.

Jamison's eyes were tight, his body was tense, yet he oozed a sense of coolness. "I'll take a Saint Arnolds and—"

"I'll take a Jamison neat, please." Cheyenne couldn't help herself.

Jamison's dark eyes were on Cheyenne's. The sides of her mouth curled up. She loved to toy with him. She didn't even care for the drink but took too much pleasure in Jamison's reaction. He waited for Nick to make the drinks before he pinched her side.

"Why do you do that? You know that drink always does you in." Jamison ran his fingers over his forehead and through his short hair. It was as if he saw a map of the night in his mind and had to figure out which route to take. Jamison always had a plan.

Cheyenne's cheeks pulled at the sides as she squirmed out of his reach. "I don't think it's the drink that does me in." She laughed. Nick placed the glasses in front of them. Cheyenne raised hers and tipped it against Jamison's.

"To us." Her green eyes were like gems in a bucket of hope with only the sun to light the way.

"Cheers." Jamison took a sip of his beer.

Cheyenne waited to make sure his eyes were back on her before she slammed back the amber liquid. It was heavy with a trail of fire along her throat. She didn't care. The effect was for Jamison, not her. Whisky was not her drink of choice, but antics, especially in public with Jamison, were better than any type of buzz she could get from the bar.

Jamison cleared his throat, which she ignored as she took off her sweater. She had on her coral-colored tank top underneath. Her stylist, Katie, had said it was the perfect color to accentuate her red hair. Cheyenne had shrugged and handed over her card. She liked Katie to make all clothing decisions. If Cheyenne had her choice, she would live in Jamison's shirts all day long. They smelled like him, and they made her feel safe. "*What could be better than that?*" she had asked Katie, who advised a lot. Advertisement deals, fans, and financial security, the list goes on and on.

"Hey, Nick, can I get another round please." Cheyenne rolled her eyes at the conversation she had earlier with Katie. Those things didn't matter. Not when you had real things to deal with. Money comes and goes, but other things don't. And some things never change. Some things that Cheyenne couldn't get out of her mind.

Jamison let out a heavy sigh. "All right." His eyes scanned the place, as if he was secret security for the president. He scoped out every inch, inspected every face, and all the exits. He waited for Nick to return with Cheyenne's drink before he got up. Jamison was very protocol, by the books. Security was always his number one focus for Cheyenne. His body moved through the room. It was not huge, but large enough for fifty people to move along the dance floor as they two-stepped to the slow vibrato of Willie Nelson.

"Hey there, Cheyenne!" A petite blond with bouncy curls squeezed her small arms around Cheyenne's shoulders.

"Oh, hey! How are you?" Cheyenne patted her back and leaned toward the bar. The woman was about her age, but lord knows Cheyenne could not place her face. Maybe it was her hair? It might have been a different color in high school. That must be it. Cheyenne shifted her focus and followed Jamison's frame as he worked his way through the crowd on the dance floor in pursuit of the jukebox. She shook her head. Of course he was going to do it. Anything to get her to slow down on the drinks. She rolled her eyes and slammed back her second drink. Jamison was like a fire that singed her throat. It was what she needed for what was about to occur. She took in a deep breath.

The blonde's mouth was in full force as she rehearsed all of the different albums she loved. Cheyenne nodded as the blonde spoke. Hopefully, there would not be a pop quiz of the order of the blonde's favorites, as Cheyenne was sure she would fail.

When the first twang of the sounds of her guitar filled the room, Jamison was at her side. "This one's for you, Cheyenne," he whispered in her ear and pulled her off the stool. She wouldn't put up a fight. Jamison was a great dancer. Even though she was not a fan of her own music, especially to dance to it. Her music was for others. She was not meant to be the person wrapped in someone's arms as they danced across a sawdust-filled floor.

Cheyenne's recorded voice filled the small bar. The sounds of velvet flickered through the speakers as the soft lights lit the room like a chorus of candles. Her lyrics played through the speakers *"Button up. Tie Me Down. Screw it back on tight. Lid is sealed."*

Jamison smiled at her. His firm grip on her small hand twirled her body in circles onto the floor. He always circled her at least twice before he pulled her back in close. His warm cologne was like home: chopped wood, bourbon, some light aftershave, bottled up into a clean scent that Cheyenne inhaled. Their boots scrapped over the scratched-up wooden floor as the alcohol eased through her veins like a zip wire of warmth. She was going to be okay.

Jamison leaned down and breathed into her ear. "Give me one more chance. I just want to dance."

"Mind if I cut in?" A deep voice from a long, long time ago crept into Cheyenne's other ear.

Her eyes spread wide open, as if she was being woken from a bad dream. She was in the Broken Spoke, in a place she never wanted to return, but Jamison's arms around her were too real. This was not a dream. The face from her past was not a faded memory that she had tried to forget.

Jamison pulled Cheyenne in tighter. With his arms around her, she was no longer frozen. She stood up straight. Her breath had been sucked from her lungs. Her chest was constricted. *Breathe.* She was okay. Jamison was there and so was Colt Clayburn.

Colt Clayburn. She hadn't seen this man in eleven years. Eleven long years. Age hadn't touched him. His skin was still full of his youthful Texas glow. His eyes were a warm honey brown that drizzled into her heart and further down to the hottest place between her thighs.

"Colt."

"Still my name. Are you still going by Cheyenne? Or did that change too?"

A tight grin fell onto his face. She wanted to kick him, but that would send off alarm bells for Jamison. Instead, she let out a stifled laugh. "No, name's the same." Her eyes met the floor. Scattered saw dust like her tattered heart, broken all over with no possible hope to reconnect. This puzzle was not meant to be finished. She knew it. Colt had to have known it too.

"Well then, Cheyenne, may I have this dance?" Colt offered his hand like a proper gentleman. Jamison's eyes glared at Colt's weathered hand as his chest flexed into a proper fighter stance from underneath a gentleman's suit. Jamison remained cool. Ice cold.

Cheyenne seemed oblivious to the chill in the room. She nodded and squeezed Jamison's hand to let him know it was okay. He gave Colt a Nordic stare before he released Cheyenne's hand, then clenched fist and returned his eyes to Colt with a glare that could only be read as "be warned."

Colt never even looked at Jamison. His focus was entirely on Cheyenne. His hands reached around her back and melded their bodies together, as if they weren't on a dance floor in front of a group of people. Like they were alone as they had been so many years before. They said nothing as he moved her around the floor. The heat of his body was doing Cheyenne in. Her throat was dry, and she could hardly breathe. She would need a glass of water after the song was over. Even though so many years had passed, the way he held her body against his was like they had never parted. A million memories of what they had shared filled Cheyenne's mind. Each trinket, each love-swept word, broken promises, and future plans were in a fight to be the prominent place of her hardest heartbreak. A wound once mistaken as being healed had opened.

As they moved, his eyes bore into hers like he was angry or hurt. She couldn't tell. Her own emotions had clouded her sight. It had been so long, and here they were together again. So much was the same and yet so much had changed. His body was larger now. No longer a teenage boy. Now he had the solid muscles of a man. His square shoulders were followed by large biceps that Cheyenne would not be able to wrap her hands around if she had wanted to. And she did. There was an urge to wrap more than her hands around his bicep. Even his scent was different, it was woodsy and of leather.

Cheyenne suddenly felt dizzy, and not because of the way he spun her around the room. It was the way he had twisted her heart in only a matter of seconds. She had to get a breath of air.

"I have to go … to the ladies." She pulled away from him, but he held her back, only long enough for her to notice it. Then he let her go.

CHAPTER TWO

Colt couldn't believe it. Cheyenne Ford was walking away from him again, her hips rocking as she made her way to the restroom. How familiar did that feel? It was kind of her thing. No goodbye this time either.

He'd spotted her as he drove past the Broken Spoke, slung over some Neanderthal's shoulder. Even in the dim light, her long red hair stood out like a beacon. For the last decade, every time he saw a woman with red hair, he thought about Cheyenne. Luckily he stopped hoping it was her after the first year. He knew she was never coming back, not to Texas, and not to him.

But tonight, when he saw her, he knew it was her. Nobody had that exact shade. No hair dye could match it, and many women had tried after Cheyenne's first album, *Broken*, went triple platinum. Everybody wanted to be Cheyenne Ford. And he couldn't blame any of them. Damn, she looked good; still the same Cheyenne, gorgeous and sexy as always, actually more so now. Her hips and breasts were fuller now, more womanly. She had curves now she hadn't had before. Maybe they could try again in another decade.

Colt ran the back of his hand over the coarse stubble of

his chin. It was late. He should get home. He was tired. He had to be up at four tomorrow like every morning. The cattle were not going to brand themselves. No good could come out of staying out. He needed to get back to Night Latch and go to bed. He had moved on. Cheyenne had moved on. She was with the massive blond guy. Colt never knew she was into blonds, but whatever. Turns out, he didn't know a lot about her.

Time to go home, old boy. If this was all it was to be, Colt would have to let it be with the dance and take things for what they were. He saw her, he held her, they danced, they sparked: carpe diem or something. Did she feel it? Because he sure as hell did. His body reacted to her the same way it always did. *Shit.* He had almost convinced himself he wasn't into her.

Colt looked over and gave her boyfriend a hard stare. Colt wanted to punch him square in the jaw. The guy was big, almost as big as Colt. They would be evenly matched. It didn't matter that it had been eleven years since Colt last saw her, his heart stilled and screamed "mine." Nope, it wasn't his heart doing the screaming, it was something lower and a lot more stupid. It would be nice to get a good fight in once in his life, really lay into someone without holding back, leveling the playing field. He would not have to hold back with this guy. The Neanderthal could take every blow and land a few of his own.

Damn it. Colt was imagining a beat-down with a guy he didn't know. Colt had no beef with this guy; clearly, he made Cheyenne happy. She smiled when she was with him and laughed. And she touched him, her hands all over him while they danced. The song playing on the jukebox was written for that guy. Colt could tell by the way Cheyenne sang the words against his cheek and the way the guy smiled and pointed to himself during the chorus.

I can't imagine you not around
Baby, I need you to stay in town
Give me one more chance

I just want to dance
Gotta have my partner
Gotta have my man
Don't leave me standing all alone

Colt's nostrils flared. This was her man. Occasionally, when he wanted to torture himself, Colt let himself wonder who she was with. Well, here he was. Now he knew, no need to speculate anymore.

Time to take it home. Colt made it as far as the door before he spun on his heel and turned back. Anger clawed at him and pushed him back into the bar. He'd had a lot of time to think about what he would say to her if he saw her again. He had said the words a hundred times before, repeated the questions he would shout at her. Sometimes when he was out in the saddle and there was nothing to keep his mind engaged, he would play out the scene. *Why did you leave? Did you ever love me? Was it the money or the fame that made you forget your roots? Is it all of Texas that isn't good enough for you? Or is it just me? Was any of it real?*

It was time for some god-damned answers.

Colt swung open the door to the ladies. Cheyenne looked up. She was bent over the sink splashing water on her face. Her big blue eyes widened at his sight. Like every part of her, they were unique, so round and dark, the darkest shade of blue, almost purple.

"Colt," she murmured as she stood.

"Still my name."

Color rose in her cheeks. Her skin was so pale, almost translucent, it glowed against the dark fire of her hair. Christ, she was beautiful.

Little drops of water dotted her top lip. Those lips that gave him his first kiss. The lips that had lied when Cheyenne and he sat in the bed of his pickup truck and planned a future together. So many lies about marriage and a family … a life with each other.

Colt opened his mouth to speak, to ask her all the

questions he had asked himself over the years, but his mind was blank. He could not think, could not see beyond her full lips. Colt moved in closer, causing Cheyenne to take a step back. She pressed her body hard against the wall, nowhere for her to go now.

Colt stared at the drops of water on the bow of her mouth, clinging to her. Christ, he was jealous of them. The things he would do to be that close to her again. Then, he gave his head a terse shake. She didn't belong to him anymore.

She had a man less than twenty feet away. A man who would be taking her home and doing all the things to her that Colt dreamed about, but she had been his first.

"Oh, fuck it. Just one for old times' sake." Colt wrapped his hands around her waist and slammed her body against his. "I'm going to kiss you." He breathed against her lips. It was her warning. If she didn't want it, she better speak up fast, because in a few seconds her mouth belonged to him.

Cheyenne didn't object. Instead, she took in a sharp breath, her breasts pushing up with the sudden intake of air. Those breasts, damn. Colt's head came down on hers. He licked the water from her top lip, savoring each drop. Salty, like tears. Had she been crying?

Her tongue reached back for his and the thought was gone. Colt sturdied himself and focused on the moment as he ran his tongue along her lips, like he wanted to remember the exact outline, and coaxed them open. His mouth melded with hers, his tongue caressing hers. So sweet, so fucking sweet and hot, just like he remembered. No ... no, it was better. His memory never captured how soft her lips were or the soft needy moan caught in her throat.

Cheyenne wrapped her arms around him, then laced her fingers through his hair, pulling him down closer.

One kiss. Just one. *She belongs to someone else.* Even as his mind screamed, his body would not listen. His mouth was on hers again, hungry and needy. He kissed her mouth, her neck, and the top of her breasts. He wanted to kiss all of her.

Cheyenne rubbed against him as he kissed her, back and forth. She was using his erection to get off, rubbing, pushing herself higher, panting with a desire like she too had yearned for him. This was not teenage lust. It was stronger. They were older now. A lot had happened since then, a lot of people. Back then, they had been so young, inexperienced. But this was like their first time all over again, except they knew what they were doing.

"The real thing would be so much better," he whispered against her ear.

Her breathing changed. She knew what he was saying. And he knew her answer. She wanted more too. This was not just a kiss. Neither of them would be satisfied with that. The craving would not be quenched until he was balls deep in her.

Colt pulled back just far enough to see her. "I don't have a condom."

"Are you clean?" Her nipples strained against her tank top, two points begging to be stroked.

"Yes. Are you?"

She nodded. "Yeah. And I'm on the pill."

Her words were the only encouragement he needed. Colt tugged her skirt up until it was around her waist and then pulled down on her satin panties, tugging them to the ground, over her boots. Next, his hands were on his zipper. In seconds, his cock was free. He did not bother pulling down his pants or his boxers. He didn't have time. There was nothing slow and sweet about this. This was a need. It was primal, two bodies that needed the other.

With a single powerful stroke, he was in her, completely sheathed by her body. He sucked in a ragged breath. So good, so tight and wet molded around him, like she was made just for him. Cheyenne's legs wrapped around his waist. He held her steady against the wall as he pumped into her over and over again until she cried out his name. Her body trembled as her inner walls contracted with powerful spasms as an orgasm swept over her. Colt stopped moving and allowed the movement of her orgasm to make him come. His balls contracted as he sprayed hot cum high into her, marking her. He closed his eyes and breathed her in, making a memory so he had something else to think about for the next ten years.

Colt kissed her neck as he slowly pulled out of her. He never wanted to leave the warmth of her body, but they were in a public restroom.

And her boyfriend was twenty feet away.

"Fuck," Colt murmured without realizing it. He just fucked another man's woman. Oh fuck.

He leaned over and helped Cheyenne with her panties, pulling them up over the red curls between her thighs, just a shade darker than her hair. So sexy. He always loved that about her. He stopped when he saw the thin white line of a scar just above her bikini line. She didn't have that before. Colt knew every part of her body.

"What's that?"

"It's my appendix scar." She pulled frantically down on her denim skirt, clearly no longer comfortable being naked in front of him.

Then, Cheyenne's eyes widened, as if the realization of what they'd just done finally struck her. His question shook off the last glow of sex. The satisfaction in her eyes turned to embarrassment and regret. The look was a blow to the chest. Colt got it. She was happy to fuck him, but she was going home with the blond guy.

Cheyenne pushed her bangs out of her eyes with the back of her hand. That's when he saw it, the tattoo on the inside of her wrist: two interlocking hearts with a "J" in the center where they joined. The lyrics of the song played back in Colt's mind, the dedication she gave on her album covers: *For J, always for you.*

Colt took her wrist and gently stroked the lines of the tattoo with his tongue. "If your boyfriend fucked you like that, you wouldn't be screwing strangers in bathrooms."

Cheyenne's mouth dropped open. "We're not strangers, Colt. I have known you my whole life."

Colt shook his head. That was the part she chose to correct, not the part about belonging to another man. Unbelievable.

"Why did you leave, Cheyenne?"

Cheyenne looked away. Tears welled in her eyes, making the sapphire irises sparkle. Her hands scrubbed at her face. "I can't. I can't do this right now." She bolted from the room.

Colt bent over and picked up the phone that had fallen out of her pocket. As he walked out of the restroom, he caught sight of Cheyenne's red locks settled against her back as she threw herself onto her boyfriend. His arms enveloped her as she buried her head in his chest.

The man looked up and glared at Colt. Murderous rage reflected in his stare. If Cheyenne was not pressed to him, the guy would have lunged at Colt. The boy was spoiling for a fight. *The feeling is mutual, buddy.*

Colt gave a derisive snort. Unbelievable. His cum was still warm in her body, and she was going home with another man.

He really should have kept on driving.

GIA STONE

CHAPTER THREE

Jamison wrapped his arms protectively around her. Cheyenne buried her head into his broad chest. What had she just done? "Take me home, J."

"The house is on Parkside. We're two minutes away." Jamison guided her out of the Broken Spoke and into the car, then put on the navigation to get to the Airbnb they rented.

Cheyenne sighed. She didn't want to go to the Airbnb. She wanted to go back to Nashville. This place was too small. Yet, it felt so big. It hurt too much, all of it. It was like she never left. Every feeling she felt then came back. Like a trap door in a haunted house. The memories were rampant, like a flood caused by a tsunami. Time had not mellowed the emotions; it had given them time to grow like those baby sponges that grow in water. Her memories were like giants in the water of her tears. Oh god, why did she come back? And then she remembered the reason, the only thing that could make her come back.

Cheyenne wrapped her arms around her legs. "You have to make it matter to make it happen," she whispered as if she was alone on a mountain with the stars, surrounded in silence. Darkness ran through her. This homecoming was for something good. It mattered. But what had she done? That had not been part of the plan. Not even back in town for twenty-four hours and she'd fallen into his arms. It was so wrong. She swallowed hard.

Jamison let his hands run through her hair and rest against her shoulder. He pulled her in with a protective embrace around her. Cheyenne didn't want to cry. She took in a deep breath. Her chest burned with the pain coiled inside her rib cage. She let out a shallow breath.

"I think Parkside is just around the corner." Jamison's voice was steady and strong.

"Yeah, just at the end of Finlay," Cheyenne muttered. He must have forgotten that she lived there for the first seventeen years of her life. The roads were the same, but everything that lined them was different. Everything had changed but the reason she had left.

"What happened in there?" Jamison's hand lifted Cheyenne's face so their eyes could meet. Anyone with a sense of empathy could see the pain packed behind her eyes. She had always been an open book with Jamison, but not about this. Not now. She wasn't ready to let all of the memories out or let him into this exact spot.

"It's just hard being back. I wish the liquor store had been open." Cheyenne broke their eye contact and rubbed her legs. They were still warm, despite the chill that ran through her mind. Tingles of regret and shame sprung in circles.

"Here it is." Jamison pulled up in front of a small Victorian at the end of the street. This was one of the houses she and Colt had always driven by and played their game of *What if*. What if they were the owners, what would they do? How would they make it better? Cheyenne smiled at the memory of her youth as she played it through her mind. They were so young and naïve. The idea of them being together past high school. Those were the days, and yet look what had happened to the house without them. Without their touch or ideas. It was hard to recognize.

The house had been completely renovated. When Cheyenne and Colt had sifted through the real estate of Cut and Shoot, it had been a wreck. Weeds had been growing through the fence and all the windows busted out. But now, it was clear someone had restored it. Purple woodwork made the gray house pop, and the pristine rose garden made it look like it belonged on a postcard, not in a one-horse Texas town.

The trunk closed hard, pulling Cheyenne back to the present. Jamison opened her door. "Come on, let's get you inside." He reached for her hand. Cheyenne slid out of her seat and onto the pavement. Jamison helped her carry their bags in. She had not brought that much, just a few pairs of jeans and T-shirts and her clothes for her concert. *I am playing Houston.* Goosebumps prickled her arms. She had vowed never to come back to Texas, and she never had.

Until now.

"You okay, princess?"

Cheyenne looked up. "I'll be fine when we cross back over the state line." She looked around at the furnishings. It was homey. The house was simple yet tastefully decorated with parquet floors and crown molding in every room. There was an open fireplace waiting to be lit if the Texas heat ever dropped low enough to warrant it.

She took her bags into the larger bedroom with the bathroom. She stripped off her clothes, hopped in the shower, and sat under the hot spray of water until she stopped crying. She didn't want to cry again in front of Jamison. He had wiped away enough tears to last a lifetime.

When she was done crying, Cheyenne got out of the shower, wrapped her hair in a towel, and put on one of Jamison's shirts. She only slept in his shirts because they made her feel safe, like he was holding her. She wiped away the steam from the bathroom and stared at her red-rimmed eyes. Tonight, his shirt wasn't going to be enough; she needed the real thing.

"J, will you sleep with me tonight?"

Jamison glanced up from the news. He switched off the TV, stood, and wrapped his arms around her again. "Of course. Take me to bed, princess."

Their hands laced. She was safe. The edge of the night had begun to wear off. It was only a few days, then they could leave and go back to their normal. This was not it.

Jamison pulled off his shirt and tossed it on the ground with his jeans. Cheyenne slid under the white duvet, pulled the comforter back, and patted the bed, inviting J in beside her. Anyone from the outside would think they were lovers. That's what Colt had thought. No one in this town would ever understand their connection.

Cheyenne snuggled deeper into the covers and faced the window. If she tried hard enough, she could also pretend she was still in Nashville.

Jamison pulled her against his chest, one arm under her, the other wrapped protectively around her. She let out the breath she was holding. Jamison wouldn't let anything happen to her. She would play the concert and then go home. She never had to see Colt Clayburn again. The thought of that robbed her of her breath.

"Who was that guy?" Jamison asked.

"Just a guy I knew a long time ago." She closed her eyes, but the fresh stream of tears would not be stopped.

CHAPTER FOUR

Colt pulled over in front of the rental property off Main Street, the place Cheyenne was staying at … not with him. Of course, they were staying in one of his properties. Colt would have realized it had the house been rented in her name, but Jamison Keyes had rented it for them, six months paid in full, even though they would not be staying more than a month. Colt had said fine by him. As long as he got paid, he didn't ask questions. He regretted that policy now. Had he known Cheyenne was staying here with her boyfriend, he would have said no. Straight up, there is no way he was okay with that.

Colt held up her phone—purple cover, her favorite color. That hadn't changed. He put in her code again. She still had the same password: 8192, the last digits of her childhood phone number. Were all her passwords the same? Doubtful, something told him her email password wasn't *ColtlovesCheyenne1* anymore.

Colt scrolled through her photos again: most were of her with Jamison, some on the road between concerts, some at her house in Nashville. There were several of them smiling and hugging, but the one that got to Colt was one of them together in bed. Jamison was bare-chested, and Cheyenne was in a T-shirt far too big for her. It's his. Colt knew it, and it infuriated him. Jamison's hand was on her ass, and she had on a goofy face as she tried to get the phone far enough away from her to get a good angle for the shot. She managed it because it left nothing to the imagination. They were in bed, smiling, probably after sex … or right before.

Christ, why was he doing this to himself?

Colt glanced up from the phone, when the front door opened. Jamison came out and ran across the street, taking off toward downtown. Colt glanced at his watch; he needed to be back in half an hour. It was a hot day, so he had brought the horses in to switch them for fresh ones. But first, he wanted to give Cheyenne back her phone. He needed to give it back just to keep from looking through her pictures and reading her texts. He wasn't a god-damned stalker; 'bout time he stopped acting like he was.

Colt stopped when he reached the front porch. Cheyenne was playing the piano, his grandma's old upright. He recognized the song. It wasn't one of her own; it was "Tennessee Waltz." That was always one of her favorites. She used to sing it to him when they danced in the bluebonnets.

When she started to sing, his breath caught in his chest. God, she had a great voice, rich and sultry, beautiful like everything about her. He loved when she sang. Did she sing this to Jamison too, Cheyenne and his song?

Colt shook his head. That was a long time ago, they didn't have a song anymore. He gave the door a hard knock.

"What did you forget?" Cheyenne answered the door with a beaming smile. It soon faltered when she saw it was not Jamison at the door. "How did you know I was here?"

"Darlin', this town has a population of less than a thousand. Do you think you were hard to find?"

She was wearing nothing but a thin white shirt. It hung just below her ass, but if she moved even slightly, he would be able to see the thatch of red curls at the top of her thighs. The thought was enough to send blood rushing to his cock.

He slid her phone back into his pocket. He didn't want to give it to her; he wanted a repeat performance of last night. A deep blush crept up her cheeks, and the way she was looking at him told him she would not need a lot of convincing.

Had he lost his fucking mind? Anger spiked in him. She was here with another man. He shook his head and asked instead, "How do you like the house?"

"It's beautiful. They did such a great job restoring it. Do you know the owner?"

Colt nodded. "I do. So do you, darlin'. You were fucking him less than twenty-four hours ago." Colt rubbed the coarse stubble along his jaw. "I probably should clarify 'cause god only knows what you got up to when you got home. The house is mine. I bought it a few years ago."

Cheyenne's cheeks went darker. "This is your house?"

Colt nodded. "Yes, ma'am, one of them. I own the old Potter Ranch. It's the Night Latch now."

Surprise showed on her pale face.

"What's wrong? Are you the only one allowed to make something of themselves? That doesn't seem fair now, does it?"

Cheyenne pulled down on her shirt like she was suddenly aware she was almost naked. No, she didn't have the right to be shy in front of him. He knew her body as well as he knew his own. He took a step forward, allowing the door to slam behind him.

Christ, she was beautiful. Why couldn't time have dampened that? She was even prettier than the day she left. She was every inch the woman now. God, he wanted her. Still. Even after the way she left, the eleven years, and seeing the pictures of her with another man. None of that mattered when he looked at her. She was still Cheyenne ... his Cheyenne.

A voice screamed at him from somewhere deep in the back of his mind, telling him he was bat-shit crazy, but it was easy enough to quiet it when he breathed in her soft scent. God, she smelled good. He wanted to smell her again and kiss her and … Oh shit, he was not thinking straight. Cheyenne had come into town like a gust of wind and separated every root he had planted when she left. Like a tumbleweed in the desert.

Yet he was skilled enough to know not to fight it, 'cause he wasn't going to win.

"Darlin', I'm not even going to pretend that I'm going to stop kissing this time." He wasn't going anywhere until he had her again. Just once more. Cheyenne's eyes met his, and she nodded. That was all he needed. She wanted it too. He ripped the shirt off her. The thin fabric moaned in protest, and then gave way. Gone, it fell from her body, all the remnants of the other man, the one she belonged to. But not right now, Cheyenne was Colt's.

Cheyenne licked her bottom lip, her tongue darting out to run along the middle. Fuck, she was sexy. Colt wrapped his hands around her waist and lifted her so he did not have to bend to kiss her. Her legs tangled behind him and her fingers laced through his hair as their mouths merged.

Colt carried her through to the bedroom, then laid them both on top of the white duvet. The feather from the soft down puffed around her hips. She was naked in front of him, all of her belonged to him right now, and he wanted to feel all of it, smell it, taste it.

Colt began dropping kisses along her neck, settling when he reached the sensitive hollow above her collarbone. He licked and kissed and sucked until Cheyenne's breath was coming in small pants.

He knew what she liked; he always had. They had discovered what felt good together. That was one of the benefits of loving the same girl your whole life. They had shared all their firsts. It started with stolen pecks in front of the locker, and then a long night of kissing under the stars. Cheyenne would rub herself against him, using his cock to come. Even separated by thick material, he could make her orgasm, but soon it wasn't enough. They both wanted more.

They wanted skin to skin.

Now, nothing less than being buried deep in her would cut it. There was no going back.

Colt's mouth dropped to her breast. He took one rosy peak in his mouth while his hand worked the other, rolling her nipple between his fingers, gently pulling. Cheyenne moaned. Her lips lifted off the bed greedily.

Colt pulled back long enough to take her in as the morning sun poured through the window. He was going to do this again: mess with another man's woman and pretend that she was his. He needed to remember this time for later. He could beat himself raw to this image; it would last a lifetime.

God, she was sexy. He needed to taste her just once. They had never done that. Cheyenne had been too shy then. Though he knew, eventually, his head would have been between her thighs. They had both wanted it too much for it to not happen.

Colt traced the scar low on her belly. His head lowered still until it hovered above the juncture of her thighs. His tongue traced the seam of her body, separating the delicate folds.

"Colt!" she exclaimed as she closed her thighs around him in a vice grip. Colt smiled against her clit.

"Colt, ahh," she squirmed.

Colt pinned her to the bed. His tongue found the sensitive nub at her core and lapped at it, tasting her.

"Ahh … Colt … What are you doing … Oh my god that feels good … Oh god, Colt."

He smiled to himself. He always knew she would love this. Her knees fell to the side, opening her further to him. He eased a finger into her and then another, stroking with the same cadence as his tongue on her clit.

"Oh my god, Colt … I have no idea what you're doing, but don't stop … Oh my god." Her body jerked under him. She was acting as if no one had ever gone down on her. Surely that couldn't be the case. What kind of man doesn't eat his woman's pussy? No wonder she wasn't satisfied.

Colt stroked faster until her moans rose to screams and finally dissolved into a contented sigh. He waited for the last tremor of her body before he pulled his long fingers from her.

Pushed himself up onto his forearms, he said, "Oh, you're not done yet, darlin'. Ready for round two?"

Cheyenne laced her fingers through his black hair and pulled him down to kiss her, giving him the answer he needed to slide into her. Could she taste herself on him? He hoped so.

Again and again, he pounded into her, taking them both higher. Cheyenne moaned into his mouth as another orgasm swept over her. She felt so good, perfect. He wanted to stay inside her forever, but he couldn't, he would not last much longer. He thrust into her again, and with a groan, he came in her, filling her.

He collapsed onto her, rolling them both onto their sides, facing each other, and kissed her. He could stay like this forever, but he needed to get back to the ranch, and ... well, she was somebody else's.

Little daggers pierced his conscience. If the roles were reversed, he would tear his balls off. Colt let out a long sigh. He needed to go.

He sat up. *She is not yours*, he reminded himself. He had pretended long enough. "Best get back to work."

Cheyenne sat up. "Um ... yeah ... um ... Jamison will be back soon." She stood and went to the bathroom.

Colt shook his head. Did she just say that to him? "I hope your boyfriend enjoys smelling me on you."

Cheyenne peeked her head out from the bathroom. Her brows pulled in, and she glanced at the floor. "Huh." She shook her head and smiled. "I am washing the sex smell off before I go out."

What was that? Was he a game to her? Did she think this was funny?

"Ah, Colt," Cheyenne shrieked from the bathroom.

"What's wrong?"

She pointed to her neck. "You gave me a hickey. We're not in high school anymore. You can't brand me like your cattle."

Colt buttoned his jeans and put his hat back on. "Darlin', if I was going to brand you, it would be here." He smacked her ass hard enough to leave a handprint.

Had he done it on purpose, the hickey? He wasn't one to leave his mark like that. What the hell was he thinking? He wasn't thinking. That was the problem. Cheyenne had moved on long ago. He needed to do the same. He couldn't pretend anymore. Cheyenne left years ago, time for him to let go.

He reached into his pocket and grabbed her phone, then punched in her passcode. The picture of her and Jamison in bed flashed on the screen. He shook his head before he handed it to her. "Enjoy the rest of your stay in Texas, Cheyenne."

Colt walked away from her without looking back. He needed to stop looking back. It was clear she wasn't.

As Colt reached for the front door, Jamison entered the house. Of course he was home. Unbelievable. Colt wanted to scream but, instead, he tilted his hat. "Howdy."

Jamison's eyes narrowed. He did not respond, probably for the best, because Colt had nothing to say that he would want to hear. Their arms brushed as Colt walked past him and out of the house. His house with his girl.

CHAPTER FIVE

Cheyenne stood under the water until it turned cold. God, that man drove her crazy. He was such a jerk now. So arrogant. Why? He used to be so sweet and loving and funny. God, he made her laugh then. Her face would ache from smiling so much. He had not made her laugh once since she had returned. He could have been a flirt with her about her phone and being back in town, but instead he was curt. There were zero jokes. Zero laughs. The only thing he had made her do was cry ... and scream ... and come.

So much sex, good sex. God, that man could move. And what he did with his tongue ... "Ahh." He was driving her crazy. No more. Once was a mistake, twice was ... amazing, but any more than that and she would need a straitjacket. This was not right. It didn't matter how good it felt. It was wrong. Very wrong.

She wrapped a towel around herself and went back to the bedroom to look for something to wear—time to put on some real clothes. Cheyenne jumped back. Jamison was in the doorway. She hadn't heard him return.

In his hand was his ripped shirt. The muscles in his jaw bunched together as he clenched his teeth, anger radiating from him.

"Was that him?" Jamison demanded. "Is he the one?"

Cheyenne took in a sharp breath. She had only seen J this angry once, and it had not ended well for the other guy. "No, no, it wasn't Colt."

"Tell me, Cheyenne," he demanded again. "Was it him? Was it the guy I just passed in the living room? The guy from last night. Was it him? Is that why you were crying?"

She shook her head. "No. No, it wasn't Colt. We go way back. We ... were ..." She didn't know what to say. She never spoke about Colt with anyone. Jamison knew there had been someone she loved, someone she'd left behind, but she never told Jamison his name or how close they were. She shut that door when she left. "He is the guy from the *Broken* album," she admitted finally. Jamison deserved the truth. That was as much as she could give him.

J's eyes widened. "Him? Really?" He let out a stream of air. "Tall, dark, and handsome was your thing then?"

She nodded. "Sorry about your shirt. I'll replace it." She prayed that he would drop the subject. She couldn't tell him any more, and J knew when she lied.

Jamison crossed the room and embraced her. "I don't give a shit about the shirt. I care about you, protecting you. Fuck the shirt." He leaned down and kissed her forehead.

"You're all sweaty." Cheyenne wiped her forehead.

"If you want to get me in the shower, princess, just ask. I'll let you join me. We both know you want to." Jamison winked at her.

Cheyenne laughed. Their relationship might be different for some to understand, but a shower together was never something they did. The jokes were for their pure entertainment.

Cheyenne's eyes danced at the silliness between them. It was clear the anger had shifted in him; they were good.

"Yeah, yeah ... you're such a tease, Jamison." Cheyenne walked back to her room. Thankfully she had brought along her full makeup caboodle for the concert. *Why would Colt do this?* She examined the bruise as she pulled out the concealer. It is so juvenile on so many levels. As she blended the cream over her skin, she let out a sigh. Hopefully, it would only last a day. She patted the area and added a few strokes outside of where the light red mark had been covered. That should work.

She pulled out her dark purple liner and ran it over the tops of her lids. This visit definitely needed some makeup, but not full country glam. It was not the right venue for that. It was going to take a lot more than makeup to get Cheyenne in the mood to be on. This would be the hardest audience for her to play.

CHAPTER SIX

This Isn't Good-bye

Baby, I won't forget you
I won't forget your cry
Baby, I won't forget you or the biggest lie

I wanted more for you
You deserved the best
How I longed to hold you against my chest

I had to let you go, even with
The smell of your neck
The sparkle of your eye
Each one of my tears is a soft lullaby
Baby, I won't forget you
Baby, you deserve more

Our fingers linked
I'm sure you winked
We'll always have this one moment; it's stolen but true
Love has always been about you

Cheyenne stroked the last chord on her guitar and gazed at Jenn's face. She was such a pretty girl. Gorgeous. Even in her pale sickly state, she was beautiful. This wasn't their first meeting. Cheyenne had been asked before to visit with Jenn. It had crushed Cheyenne to find out about Jenn's condition, that she had been admitted to the hospital again. Cheyenne had hopped on the first plane to see her, canceled a sold-out show in Nashville at the Wildhorse Saloon. It didn't matter. Nothing mattered when it came to Jenn.

Cheyenne reached forward and squeezed her hand. It was soft and sweet, like Jenn. Dammit, why did she have to be in the hospital? Why? Why couldn't Cheyenne be in her place? Not to be a martyr. Just to make sure Jenn wasn't here. Jenn deserved so much more. Even this room wasn't good enough for her. It was cold and stark. Why couldn't hospital rooms have a bit more cheer or hope? Instead of the bleached-out walls and empty stands, full of machines that beep. And cords, so many cords. Not the kind you play but the ones you hope will keep you playing on. Let your life continue. Or the person in the bed. A hospital bed. One of the worst places a person can be or sit next to. Other than the alternative. It was not a place to be. *Ever.*

"Do you want me to sing you another one?" Cheyenne's eyes held back a river full of tears. She had made a promise to never cry in front of Jenn. On the car ride home, when she was safe with Jamison, then she would let the tears flow, mess up her makeup and splatter her face with red splotches. That would be okay. Everything was always okay with Jamison. He would wrap her up in his big, strong arms and hold her while he stroked her hair.

"Would you play 'Sunset on Us'? That's one of my favorites. I know it's sad"—Jenn glanced out the window for a second—"but I think that's why I like it."

Cheyenne's chest tightened. She never sang from her *Broken* album. Everyone knew that. Jenn probably knew this as well. She was a bright girl for the age of ten, even though she was stuck in a hospital bed. Her days most likely consisted of hope and boredom, so she probably had her taste in social media and had read the tabloids. Cheyenne never promoted that album. She'd turned down a seven-figure tour deal, saying she appreciated it and hoped they would be interested in her second album. She just couldn't sing any of the songs from *Broken*. Not in a small venue, not in a large sold-out stadium, not to herself. Those songs had been written, recorded, and forgotten.

Fortunately, her second, third, and fourth albums had also been well-received, and she was offered more tours. More deals. But that didn't stop the requests. People loved *Broken*.

The bangs against Cheyenne's forehead were heavy against her. A monitor beeped in the background, bringing her back to the present. So many machines. Jenn was so young and had already gone through so much. Too much. This just wasn't fair. It made Cheyenne question everything. Her choices. Her faith. Her resolve. Her own personal convictions. It didn't matter how many different ways she ran through the scenarios in her mind. Jenn being in this hospital bed did not make sense.

How much longer would it take for them to find a match? Cheyenne didn't understand with the number of medical advancements in the last twenty years that there wasn't a donor available for Jenn. One freaking bone marrow donor. That's all she needed. That's why Cheyenne was back. She was going to find a donor for Jenn, no matter what it took or what efforts or pain Cheyenne had to go through to make it happen. Cheyenne was determined. And just like her fiery red hair, when her mind caught a flicker of a flame about an idea, she didn't stop until a wildfire was set.

That's when it hit her. If Jenn could manage her treatment protocol, all the needles, all the surgeries, the injections and hopeful possibilities that ended in another empty option with no results, Cheyenne could manage a song. She could do it. She would do it for Jenn. There was no way she could deny this simple request. Cheyenne was determined to lessen the pain of the hospital experience for Jenn in any way that she could. Her own pain was not a consideration.

"Sure, sweetie. Anything you want." Cheyenne plucked a few of the notes and began to sing the soft melody. She was a true performer, and her voice didn't falter. She didn't miss a beat or skip a note. Everything about the song was perfect, except for her insides. The wounds of her painful memories had been splintered open, and with each lyric, a flood of vinegar came down and poured over the cuts of her soul. Everything she had lost. Everything that she had been through, all of it came shooting up to the surface like a volcano of emotions in her heart. Lava trickled down her veins. Little fires that seeped through each vessel.

Cheyenne ignored the pain like a mercenary in the heat of battle and focused on the chords strummed in tune with her soft voice. No pain could keep her from a promise to Jenn. The song was like a drop of hope for Cheyenne to offer. It was small, tiny, like the little fingers that grasped her hand ten years ago. So tender and sweet.

The sides of Cheyenne's mouth raised, and she focused on Jenn and her dark black hair. She had soft ringlets and both ears had light blue studs that shined just like Jenn's warm brown eyes. Such a pretty girl.

"But, baby, I had to be free." Cheyenne left the last note hanging in the air. Even the hospital machines seemed to silence from the song. All eyes were on her. She flashed a grin she didn't feel. Cheyenne knew when and how to put on a smile, and this was one of those moments.

Jenn's mom, Maggie, dabbed at her eyes from the corner of the room. She was a good mom, older than most, as the silver streak in her dark bob testified to it, but she was so devoted. Jenn was loved.

"Thank you," Jenn said, "I love that song." Her eyes sparkled like she had received a special dolly on Christmas morning.

Cheyenne smiled back and stood up. She ran her hands over the girl's hair. If she only knew.

"Sweetie, I've got to go. They said I could only stay an hour today."

Jenn's mouth formed a pout. "Okay. Will you come again? Please?"

"Sure, I will come back real soon. Maybe next time you can sing with me?"

Jenn's eyes sparkled. "That would be so cool!"

Cheyenne reached down and kissed the top of Jenn's head. A lump caught in the back of her throat, and she blinked away a tear before it surfaced.

In the hallway, Jamison grabbed her hand and squeezed it—he knew what these meetings meant to her—and led her down the long corridor. The smell of bleach surrounded them. The stare of nurses pressed into her skin as she walked by. It was obvious that they recognized Cheyenne but had been warned not to speak to her. The whispers behind their hands were confirmation. Normally she would stop and smile real big, maybe pose for a few pictures, but today was different. She needed to get out and fast. She did her best to avoid eye contact and focus on her steps. Thankfully, Jamison was a professional in every way. He guided her out of the hospital with sheer focus and speed.

As they approached the car, he opened the door for her and helped her into the passenger seat. If she didn't put up a protest, he would buckle her in. Everything Jamison did was to make sure Cheyenne was safe and taken care of. Despite this, being in the hospital was almost too much for Cheyenne to deal with. Her chest was like a fire with singed skin that traced around her lungs. She could breathe once they were out of the parking lot.

"I'm concerned about the concert," Jamison said, his eyes focused on the road.

Cheyenne jerked her head back. Jamison was never concerned with things. Or if he was, he wouldn't let on. And definitely, not to Cheyenne.

"About what?" Cheyenne glared at Jamison's biceps. They bulged through his shirt. He must have worked his upper body today. Cheyenne let her eyes run up to his neck. His jugular vein was in full pulsation mode. This was not good.

"Security. We need to have more people. The Houston crowd can get a little out of hand. Your last album crossed over into the pop market, and that brings a mix of characters." He merged onto the highway as if he was in a getaway car. No traffic laws were broken, but his moves were not his standard smooth disposition.

"Was there another letter?" The hairs along the back of her neck pricked up. It had been at least a month since the last one had been received. The police were still on the case, but Cheyenne had her doubts about what that meant. So far nothing had happened, but that didn't stop the visual of the words that flashed through her mind. Jamison had tried to keep it from her, and would have been successful had Katie not seen it in the mailbag and shown it to her. They'd both screamed. It was so nasty. Jamison had run into the room, furious. This was the third letter. The other two had already been handed over to the police.

"I want to up the security."

Cheyenne's chest tightened. "Was it like the other one?"

"Do you want me to swing through Taco Bell? I saw there is a one near Main Street."

"J, come on. I'm a big girl; I can handle it. Tell me." She grabbed onto his bicep. It was flexed and hard, and he wasn't doing it for show. It was just the way he was made. The man was a muscle machine. He put *Men's Fitness* covers to shame.

"Princess, Taco Bell or Chipotle? I'm in the mood for Chipotle." He shrugged. "And I'm driving, so Chipotle it is."

Cheyenne let out a sigh. "They don't serve Diet Pepsi at Chipotle."

"Since you're looking so pretty over there, I'll swing into

a gas station and grab you a bottle." He winked at her. His light green eyes always flickered when he flirted with her.

Cheyenne laughed. "You're too much."

"Of a good thing." He glanced over at her. His eyes always made the world seem warmer, even in a stark moment.

Jamison steered the Escalade to a gas station and hopped out. His solid body passed through the doors. Cheyenne smiled and shook her head when the woman coming out of the gas station turned to give Jamison a second glance, no doubt in admiration of the view from behind. The man did have a nice ass.

As she waited for Jamison to be done, Cheyenne pulled up her Twitter account. She tried her best to keep up with social media, but there were so many avenues. She liked to meet her fans at the concerts and behind the stage, maybe send a few emails here and there, but social media was out of her scope. Other than a quick check-in on a few classmates and celebrities. Cheyenne rarely posted anything herself. She didn't understand it and didn't care to figure it out. It was too much—Twitter, YouTube, Pinterest, Facebook, Instagram, Tumblr … the list went on. She would post a greeting message to the city she happened to be in, but, usually, she stayed away from it at all costs.

The lump from before grew in her throat as she spotted the trending hashtag. Despite her small knowledge of social media, she understood what trending topics meant. But what she didn't understand was why her timeline was full of words that were all about her and Jenn.

#Broken #CheyenneFord #SunsetOnUs #HospitalGirl #CheyenneSings #ThisIsntGoodbye #TexasChildrensHospital #CheyenneIsUnBroken #CheyenneHospitalGirl

Cheyenne's eyes fell out of her head. Every single trending topic was about her. How? Why? Yes, she sang from *Broken*, but how did Twitter and the rest of the world know? This didn't make sense.

As her eyes focused on all the hashtags, the car door

opened. Jamison leaned into the car and switched her phone out with the Diet Pepsi.

"I already saw."

"You saw the video?" The vein in his jaw flexed.

"What? There's a video?" Cheyenne tried to grab her phone back.

"Yes, one of the nurses recorded you." His lips formed into a solid frown.

Cheyenne's heart sank. *Oh god.*

CHAPTER SEVEN

Cheyenne had no appetite after she watched the covert video from the hospital at least twenty times. Not to listen to herself sing. But to see Jenn. Being able to view Jenn as she looked up at Cheyenne while she sang was surreal. How many times had she imagined being able to sing to Jenn? The video was an invasion of privacy, especially to Jenn and her family. But Cheyenne was infatuated with it. She looked up how to save the video outside of Twitter, so she had her own copy. She could pull it up whenever she wanted and watch Jenn. It was perfect.

Jamison seemed hungrier than normal and finished Cheyenne's food too. He was ravenous. Too much energy was in his body. He was clearly upset. He never fiddled, but he crossed and uncrossed his legs at least five times while he ate. After that, he began to roll his neck a few times and pop his knuckles but gave Cheyenne an excuse about how midday exercises are the newest rage and how he needed to burn off some calories. He tried to get Cheyenne to go with him, but she was not up for a run. She wanted to be alone.

Once Jamison left, images of Colt and his hat and his mouth and his hands all over and inside her body would not stop. *Over and over again.* Too many times. Too many ways.

She lay down in her bed with the door closed and pulled down her panties, letting her hand find the special spot. She was good at this. Sometimes she challenged herself to how many orgasms she could give herself in one event. Her record was ten. Maybe she could pass that number today, but ten was such a solid number. It was like she had won something … and she had, ten moments of pleasure. Granted, they were all alone, but there was no heartbreak or fear with her hand, just the zing of the lightning that ran down her arms and legs. When it reached her toes, she knew it was a good one, but all those orgasms had not even compared to what Colt had given her. Damn, he'd given her so many orgasms in the past two days that shattered any record she held on her own. She had not seen the sparks alone that she had experienced with him. The bar had been raised. Cheyenne couldn't compete with Colt and his mouth or his hands, and surely not with his cock.

This pissed her off. It was not going to happen. She pulled her panties back on. She had promised Jamison she wouldn't leave, but she was a grown woman with a bone to pick. It was time Colt knew that she didn't appreciate him and all his orgasms. Not when he was such a jerk about it. They had too much history. Cheyenne thought it would remain in the past but, obviously, that was not the case. Colt was clearly confused about her current relationship status. Maybe she should have clarified. Yet, Colt made it difficult to be vulnerable. How was she ever going to be able to open up to him?

She backed out of the driveway like her house was on fire and she needed to get away before it exploded. Jamison had, of course, run to the gym. He ran more miles in a day than Cheyenne would run all year. That was not her thing. She loved how healthy Jamison was, but there was no way she could meet him on any physical level.

As the tree-lined roads gave way to golden fields that stretched onto the horizon, Cheyenne begrudgingly admitted that Texas was beautiful.

She turned up the dirt road that led to Night Latch. Sure enough, Colt was with a bunch of cattle. Good thing he was alone; she didn't want anyone to overhear what she was about to say. It needed to be said. He was too arrogant and cocky for his good. The passion they had meant something, but his terse demeanor made the silver lining of hope turn into a Negative Cloud-to-Ground Lightning. The bright spark that looks like it has a sharp target in the sky, but in reality, it shoots downward and touches the ground. He had changed, and it wasn't for the better. His spark used to go somewhere, and now it just shut down. This could be fixed. *Maybe.* Cheyenne was no engineer. But she knew Colt. Or she had.

Cheyenne hopped out of the Escalade and marched to where Colt stood. His sleeves were rolled up past his elbow, exposing the tanned skin on his heavily muscled forearms. Unlike Jamison, who built his muscles at the gym, Colt's were earned through hard manual labor.

Colt wiped the sweat from his brow with one hand, as if making sure it was her that he was seeing. His eyes sparkled back at her. Nope. Not going to happen. He needed to keep his sparkles to himself. This was not going to end in sex. No matter how much she had wanted it. No.

"Colt, we need to talk." She pressed her lips together. *Wait, be cool, don't let emotions get wrapped into this conversation.*

"Is that right, darlin'?"

"Yes, listen here. You can't come over anymore." She tapped his chest with her finger.

Colt's face sunk for a moment, and then he raised an eyebrow. "I think we might have a problem with that now, don't you think?"

Cheyenne's eyes squinted. Of course. How clever.

"It doesn't matter that you own the place. Just don't come back anymore." She let her eyes meet the dirt. "Just not while I'm still in town." She nodded with assertion.

He reached for her hand and pulled her body into his hard muscular chest. Leather and wood mixed with his sweat swarmed around her. "You and I both know that you are dishing out a bucket of lies. You want me to come back, just like you want me to take you right here and now on my land." He leaned down and bit her neck.

She shrieked and pulled back. "Colt, you can't do that. Why do you have to be such a jerk? You used to be so sweet." Her eyes filled for a second, and she quickly cleared them. There was no way she was going to show an ounce of sadness in front of Colt and all his cockiness. She needed to be strong. She could do this.

"Then why did you leave?"

Cheyenne cut their eyes. She wasn't ready for this conversation. She was here to tell him not to be such a jerk, not to address their past. Over the years, she had imagined what it would have been like, but then she popped open a bottle and let the liquid silence her memories and any possibility of Colt.

"Oh, I know, this place wasn't good enough for you. Is that it? You needed more. I guess you got it, except for the sex part. 'Cause Jamison isn't satisfying you."

Cheyenne was almost about to be hurt, and then he mentioned Jamison. That's when she let the laughter fall from her mouth. It was comical that he continued to bring him up. She blinked and smiled a big grin. On purpose. Her grin could silence any of his cockiness. She needed to tell him the truth about Jamison. She had to. But it was clearly something that bothered him. So it would have to wait, just a little bit longer.

Colt's eyebrows crinkled. "You've changed."

The sides of her mouth shrunk. "Not as much as you."

"I might have made a mistake, maybe a couple, but I'm not going to do it again. I don't mess with Texas, and I sure as hell am not going to continue to mess with another man's woman." He put his hands in his pockets, almost as if it was an attempt to make a barrier between them.

"What are you talking about?" Her eyes squinted at him. The glare of the sun behind him created a halo around his head, making him look like an angel, a fallen angel. Ha, but he was no angel, and he was wrong about her. Well, only on some things. And especially about Jamison. Which was funny. Heck, he might even find it funny, if he knew. But not yet. She would let him remain bothered.

"Maybe I need to talk to him. What you are doing isn't right. You're better than that, Cheyenne, or at least you used to be." His hands dug deeper into the worn denim.

That burned. Deep. She was better than a cheater. Cheyenne's cheeks warmed. No, Colt didn't know what he was talking about. "Who?" She breathed, almost too soft to hear. Her throat cut inside. The idea that Colt would ever think she was a cheater was awful. But she needed to play along with his nonsense for a little longer. She wasn't ready to come clean. His false assumptions were almost bigger than his arrogance … almost.

"Jamison, your boyfriend or whatever he is to you."

"Go for it. I'd love to watch, so you be sure and get me a front-row ticket. VIP if you can afford it with your new-found wealth and all."

She tossed her hair over her shoulder and hopped back into her car, then spun off the dirt road with so much throttle it kicked up enough of a haze to make Colt look away. That's right, look away, baby, because you don't have a clue.

GIA STONE

CHAPTER EIGHT

Cheyenne eyed the numbers. How many times had she studied these papers? And for what purpose? Reading them again wasn't going to change anything. The figures wouldn't be altered anytime soon, at least not soon enough to make a difference for Jenn. Cheyenne let out a sigh. Besides, she had all these digits memorized. She even went over them in her head to a rhythm that she would never record into a song. That would be a beat she would not ever want to hear out loud. It was already too loud in her mind.

Her shoulders slumped. Seventy percent of patients have to find a compatible bone marrow transplant donor from a stranger. That was a big number. She bit at the inside of her cheek. It didn't matter. Cheyenne made a promise to herself and a silent one to Jenn.

She placed the papers back in her folder and stuck them in her purse. With the straps on her shoulder, she passed in front of the mass of sweaty muscles on the floor. Jamison was shirtless doing one-armed push-ups. *Dayum, the man was a pure machine.* "You want me to sit on your back for a little extra effort?"

"You don't weigh enough to be defined as extra effort." He breathed his words with a casualness that made him seem even more unreal.

"I could try and walk on your back and work on my balancing skills?" Cheyenne spun on her toes.

Jamison hopped up. "Not again. Last time I was a second away from letting you slip to the floor."

Cheyenne laughed. "Awe, J, you'd never let me fall."

"Exactly, that's why we aren't doing that again." He gulped back the bottle of water in his hand. "Are you going somewhere?"

Cheyenne glanced at the window in the room. A picturesque view she could appreciate in any other state but here, and not with the mission at hand. "Yeah, I'm just going to ask if Colt will register. I don't want to. But he might be the match for Jenn."

"Do you want me to go with you? I'll have to shower first." He winked at her.

Cheyenne giggled. "No, sweaty boy. I can handle this on my own. I'm not going to stop anywhere but his place."

"All right. Call me if anything happens. I haven't done any sprints today, so I'm locked and loaded for a good run."

"When isn't that the case, J?" She kissed his cheek, and he swatted her behind before she closed the door. Jamison opened it back up and waited until she was safe in the car before he went back inside.

CHAPTER NINE

Colt scowled when the barbwire caught on the pocket, another shirt ripped. He took it off to inspect the damage and only then realized he was bleeding. There was a small gash along the flat plane of his stomach. He would live. He took off his hat and wiped the sweat from his brow. It had been a long day, and he was ready for a shower and a beer.

A black Escalade pulled up in the distance. Cheyenne. Or Jamison. Part of him wished it was Jamison, so they could just get it done with. That fight was going to produce more blood than the scratch on his belly, but it would be worth it. He hated the guy, straight-up hated him.

His fists clenched, almost as tight as his jaw. The flash of Cheyenne's hair as it swung from the outside of the car door softened his armor, though other body parts began to harden as she marched toward him.

"Evening." Colt tipped his hat to her. Her hair hung past her waist in loose red curls.

Cheyenne bit into her lip as if she needed to consider what to say.

"Change your mind about not coming around, I see," he offered when she didn't immediately say anything.

Cheyenne tilted her head to the side. "Don't be a jerk.

There is something I need to talk to you about." Her gaze went to his bare chest and then lower, settling just below his belt buckle. The desire in her eyes was clear as day. A chat was never going to be what she wanted from him.

"Seems to me we haven't been much for talking since you got back. You must save the talking for somebody else, but you come to me for what I am good at." She wanted him for one thing. If he were a better man, it would bother him more, but he wasn't, not when it came to Cheyenne. He wanted to be. But something about her made it impossible for him to be the man he thought he should be. With her, he would take any part she offered.

Cheyenne rubbed her lips together. "Colt, you have no idea what you're talking about."

"Don't I? You fuck me and you go home to him. It seems pretty clear."

"You have no idea, do you? Oh, Colt. I love Jamison, I do. He has been the only man in my life for a long time, but—"

"But what? You still come around here looking for a good, hard ride. That's not love, darlin'. You're smart enough to know that. You can't claim to love one man and fuck another." He wiped his brow with the ripped shirt.

Anger and indignation flashed in her dark blue eyes. "You know what, Colt. I am smart. Smart enough to realize I don't owe you an explanation. My life is my business."

Anger mounted in him. "Why are you here, Cheyenne?"

Her nostrils flared. He knew she wanted to yell at him. She could always give as good as she got. "I am playing a charity gig in Houston next weekend."

"So I've heard. Cheyenne Ford is back, playing her first-ever concert in Texas. I watch the news."

"Yeah. Tickets are free. All you have to do is register to be a bone marrow donor."

Colt nodded. Why was she telling him all this? Everyone in Texas knew about this.

"I think you should register." Cheyenne looked down at

her feet, then back up at him. "I mean, everyone should. It is a good cause."

Colt shoved his gloves in his back pocket. "Yes, it is."

"So you're going to register? There will be a mobile registration unit there. I happen to know the singer so I can get you an early appointment." Her deep blue eyes sparkled at him. What was it that she wanted?

"No, ma'am. I won't be needing that."

The smile slipped. "Why? You just agreed it was a good cause."

"'Cause I already registered last week when I gave blood. Don't need tickets to a fancy concert to do the right thing."

Her eyes widened. "Oh … wow … well … that is great. Yeah … great cause."

"Yes, ma'am, it is. You could have called me to ask. Number's still the same as it was when you left."

A blush crept up her neck. She was wearing the same outfit as the night in the Broken Spoke: a denim skirt that showed off her great legs and a tank top that showed just enough cleavage to hold the interest of any red-blooded man.

God, she was hot. Colt dropped his pliers. He wrapped an arm around her waist and pulled her against him. "You don't need to make up excuses to see me, darlin'," he whispered into her hair. Her body was soft and supple, molding against him.

"Colt," she whispered breathlessly. "We shouldn't."

"Nope, we shouldn't. But we are." He leaned down and captured her mouth with his. She was so sweet, the way her body yielded to him and sighed into his mouth.

"Colt." She pulled away, taking a step back. "We both know this is wrong, so wrong. It could never work between us. So no quick, frantic, needy, hot sex. I have amazing willpower. No, stop smiling, I do. Ask me what my favorite smell of all time is?"

Colt's lips curled into a smile. "The smell of me on you? Is that why you keep coming around?"

Cheyenne rolled her eyes and sighed. "Cheeseburgers. My favorite smell is cheeseburgers. Sometimes I go into fast food joints just to smell them, even though, as you know, I have been vegan since I was eleven."

"Yep, I know, the only vegan in town, and you loved a cowboy. Always was one for irony." He nuzzled into her neck and licked it. He wouldn't leave another mark. She had asked him not to, and he would respect that.

Cheyenne smiled. "My point, Cowboy, if you will stop interrupting me, is that I know I would love a cheeseburger. Love it. Marry it and have its babies. But I won't, because I don't believe in it. Iron will." She pointed at herself with both thumbs.

"I like where this story is going. I'm the meat you want to eat." Colt laughed as he pretended to undo his zipper.

"Exactly! Now take your hands away from your pants, boy," Cheyenne scolded.

"Because you want to do it." His face hurt from smiling. It felt good to tease her again, like flexing a forgotten muscle.

Cheyenne held up her hands in exasperation. She was beautiful when she was frustrated, angry, sad, happy, and excited. She was just beautiful.

"Darlin', you are in charge of where this goes. Just say the word and we move forward, we stop, or we take a step back. It's up to you." Colt took her hand and kissed it.

"I don't want to go in the past or to stop. But you need to know some things before we move forward." Cheyenne took a deep swallow, then smoothed down her skirt.

"Jamison is not my boyfriend. I'm not some cheater that you have made up in your mind. He's my bodyguard and manager."

"Bodyguard and manager?" Colt laughed. "Is that the term for 'friends with benefits' in Nashville?"

Cheyenne laughed. Her cheeks turned bright red. "Colt, you are completely absurd, and you're misjudging me in this instance."

"Cheyenne, I see the way he looks at you. Hell, what red-blooded man wouldn't look at you like that?" Colt ran his hands through his hair. He hated to speak about another man to Cheyenne.

"A gay man." Cheyenne's voice was quiet, as if she had shared a secret.

"What?" Colt dipped his head in closer. He must have misheard.

"Jamison is gay." Cheyenne eyed the ground. "Please don't speak about it. That's his business, not anyone else's to discuss."

"Darlin', I don't care who he wants to screw as long as it isn't you." Colt pulled her in close. "Now that we have that settled. Do you want to continue?" He licked his lips. In reality, he wanted to lick hers.

Cheyenne nodded. "Yes." That's all he needed to hear. One word to confirm she was ready to go.

Colt carried her across the field and into the barn. Gently, he laid her in the hay and looked into her eyes. "This is wrong. We don't belong together anymore, not after what you did. But it will still be wrong tomorrow, so right now I am going to make you feel good."

Cheyenne didn't say anything; she just stared at him wordlessly, acknowledging the truth.

"Take off your clothes," Colt commanded.

"Cowboy, you better simmer on the commands. I might like a decisive man, but not a rude one."

"I apologize." Colt glanced at the straw, then back at Cheyenne. Damn, she was absolutely gorgeous. How many times had he fantasized about her being with him in this barn? "Cheyenne, will you bestow upon me the honor of seeing your naked skin?"

Cheyenne's chest rose and fell in shallow breaths. "Okay." She held up her hands and allowed him to pull her shirt off. It was stained with his blood; he had marked her again.

"Keep going." Colt stood back. "Please." He was really

going to have to work on this whole manners thing. Slowly, she undid her bra and laid it beside her in the hay. "And your skirt. Take it off. Take it all off. I want you naked." He licked his lips. "Please," he added again. Manners.

Wordlessly, she complied, slipping her panties over her hips. She was naked in front of him. His breath caught in his chest. His gaze traced the lines of her body, from the soft curve of her hip to the pink tips of her breasts. The areolas were so pale, almost blending in with the rest of her skin, but her nipples were darker, like the flesh of a ripe berry. Perfect. All women should look like this. Much to his chagrin, they didn't. He had gone through a lot, searching for one who looked like her, smelled like her, and cried out like she did when he made her come. No one was Cheyenne.

"Give me your hands."

Her eyes narrowed. "Why?"

"Because I am going to have you the way I have dreamed of since you left."

She took in a sharp breath. For a moment time stopped, and she did not move. But then she nodded. Colt took the rope from his belt and wrapped it around her wrists. Once, twice, three times he wound it before he tied it off with a knot. "Don't pull on the binds. Your skin is too delicate. If you ever want me to stop, just say so. But don't say it unless you mean it, because if I stop, we're done. Do you understand?"

Cheyenne nodded.

"No, say the words."

"I understand."

"And you want it, everything I am going to do to you. All my fantasies. Tell me you want it."

Cheyenne gulped. He was asking her to agree to it blindly. It wasn't fair. But her leaving wasn't fair. "Yes. Yes, I want it." Her pupils were dilated, the blue almost entirely engulfed by the obsidian center.

"I'm going to make you regret leaving. You made a bad choice, Cheyenne," he said ominously.

"Colt—" She blinked, clearly scared. It couldn't be about this moment. There was something deeper that etched in her features. He would have to figure that out later.

"Say no, and I stop," he reminded her. "But if you don't, you're mine. All of you. Every way I want."

She closed her eyes and nodded.

Colt brushed his hands over her skin. He kissed underneath her ear, then his tongue dipped into the hollow of her neck. Slowly he traced a path to her nipples, rolling them in between his fingers until her back arched. So beautiful ... and his ... not to keep ... but for right now.

His hand ran up her leg and settled between her thighs. His thumb found her clit between the red curls. With a feather-light touch, he stroked her, gently, over and over in small circles around the sensitive peak. Cheyenne raised her hips to meet his hand, urging him to stroke harder, faster, but he wouldn't.

This was his fantasy, watching her turned on, aroused but never satisfied. The way he had not been fully satisfied since she left. She would beg.

Her skin glowed, pink and slick as the evidence of arousal built in her. He increased the pressure, pushing her higher. Her head fell to the side as she moaned his name. "Right there ... please ... Ahh, Colt."

"Tell me you shouldn't have left," he rasped.

Cheyenne squeezed her lids together. She didn't speak.

"You always were my wild mare. No one ever broke you, did they? But that's what you need. You need broken, Cheyenne."

Colt took the spur from his boot and pressed the metal against the sensitive flesh of her breasts. "Ahh," she moaned as the spikes worked into her skin. Her expression straddled the line of pleasure and pain. Her skin turned red as he traced a path across her body, over her breasts and the soft curve of her hips and belly. He crisscrossed over her skin until pink tracks lined her pale skin. Her breasts rose and fell as her breath came in shallow pants.

Again he returned to her pussy, massaging her lips and circling the moisture around the opening of her body, dipping the tip of his finger into her to sample her wet heat before pushing his finger all the way into her with shallow thrusts. He rubbed her everywhere, feeling and exploring, nothing was off-limits except her clit, because that is where she wanted him to touch. But this wasn't about her satisfaction. He could make her come in seconds; he had done it countless times before. This was about desire and denial.

"Colt, please," she begged.

Colt shook his head. She wasn't tamed. As soon as the gate was open, she would bolt. She needed saddled and reigned in. "What do you want, Cheyenne? Tell me."

"Colt, please." She pulled against the coarse binding of the rub. The skin on her wrists was red and raw. She would draw blood if she kept pulling.

"You said no more fast, needy sex. I promised you slow. This is what you wanted, isn't it, darlin'? Nice and slow."

Cheyenne groaned. "Fast is good. Hard and fast. Colt, please, I changed my mind. I like it fast." The frustration in her voice. She wanted it deeper.

Colt leaned down and kissed her. "You know I am a man of my word. If you ask for slow, I'm going to give you slow."

His hand continued to stroke her, never giving her enough pressure, always holding back. He watched her chest rise and fall. If it got too quick, she was getting close to coming, so he eased off. Over and over he repeated the cycle, each time taking her slightly higher.

"Ahh," she screamed. "I hate you. You're torturing me."

"Tell me you shouldn't have left," he said again.

Cheyenne pushed her hip up against him, riding his hand. "Please," she begged. "I need you inside me."

"Where do you need me?"

"In me. Please."

Colt lowered his head until he hovered above her thighs. "Is this where you want me, darlin'."

"Yes! Yes. Please." She gasped. "Please make love to me, Colt. I need you."

Satisfaction spread through his chest. They were the words he wanted to hear. He rewarded her by lowering his head to the entrance of her body. He then spread her legs wide so she was open to him, fully exposed. Her pussy was pink and wet, glistening, ready for him, only him. *Mine.* He licked her. His tongue entered her body, making love to her like she had asked ... no, begged. The proof of her desire was salty on his tongue. Her taste, the one he loved.

Cheyenne rocked her hips against him, meeting every thrust of his tongue. Her legs jerked as frenetic energy built between her thighs. She was going to come.

Only if he let her.

He pulled back again. "Tell me you shouldn't have left."

"Yes. Yes. I shouldn't have left. I should never have left you. I need you, just you."

Pride swelled in him. He rewarded her by returning to her clit. He sucked and licked as his fingers spread her, circling her inner walls.

"Oh, God, yes. Yes, Colt, yes. Don't ever stop. Please don't stop," she screamed out as her orgasm rocked her body. She thrashed against her binding as wave after wave of pleasure rocked her.

Colt held her until the last tremors had faded from her body and her breathing had returned to normal. "That is how a man should do it," he said against her ear.

Cheyenne opened her eyes. "You were always my man, Colt. Always."

The words he always wanted to hear. Colt undid the rope to free her hands and kissed the angry red marks on her wrists. So delicate.

He took her face in his hands and kissed her. God, she felt good, so right. Slowly, he eased his cock into her, savoring each sensation, every sigh, every movement in case this was their last time. That was always more than a possibility with them. Would he want to know when it was their last time? Would it make it better? Would he have not been as bitter if he had known back then that it was their last time? No. No matter what, he would want more, always, forever.

"Cheyenne," he breathed her name like a benediction.

Her hands laced through his hair, bringing his head lower to deepen the kiss, the movements of their tongues matching the gentle cadence of their hips.

Cheyenne moaned into his mouth as another orgasm spread through her body. He wanted it to last, stay intimately connected to her forever. But it was too good, too much, so sweet.

He came inside her with a groan. Damn, she was so perfect, this ... them ... the way it should be.

Colt rolled them to their side, still inside her. He held her for a long time, neither of them speaking. Words could only ruin it, shatter the fragile connection.

Eventually, he did need to pull out of her. The reality was a bitch. They both had their own lives to return to, and responsibilities.

He handed Cheyenne back her clothes. She would leave now. Nothing had changed.

"Would you like to stay for dinner?" he asked before he could stop himself. She would say no. *Don't give her the chance to reject you again.*

Cheyenne surprised him by smiling. "What vegan food do you have, Cowboy?"

"I'll have you know I was planning on having a salad tonight."

"With your steak."

"Obviously." He smiled.

"That's the cowboy I know. I would love to have a salad with you."

"I also have peanut butter and raspberry jam."

Cheyenne's smile widened. "You know that's my favorite. Cowboy, you already seduced me, no need to bring your A-game now. Save that for later."

"If I had only known it would take a PB&J."

Cheyenne leaned forward and kissed his cheek. "I love your stubble."

"Then I will never shave again."

Cheyenne shook her head and laughed. "No, you're far too handsome to cover that face with a beard."

He grabbed her hands and kissed her wrists and welts. "I'll take you back to the house, and then I will see to the horses."

Cheyenne shook her head. "I'll come with you."

Colt shot her a dubious glance. "You want to clean the stable."

"Cowboy, take that surprised look off your face. I was born and raised in Cut and Shoot, Texas. I know how to muck out a horse."

"I know how to do a lot of things. That doesn't mean I would volunteer to do them."

Cheyenne stood up and pulled her tank top over her denim skirt. "Why is it so hard to believe I would want to help you clean the stables? I want to spend some time with you, not on my back." She held up her hand to stop him from speaking. "Not that I'm complaining. The time I have spent on my back has been amazing. But I miss talking with you."

"Woman, we both know you only think my mouth is good for one thing, and it ain't talking."

Cheyenne stood on her tiptoes and kissed his cheek again. "That's not true, Cowboy. You're a great kisser. Don't forget that. I need your mouth for that too."

Colt circled her fingers with his hand and led her to the stables. They worked side by side, cleaning and laying fresh hay, Cheyenne humming a tune he did not recognize. He knew all her songs. He would never admit it, but he had all her albums.

"Looks good, right?" Cheyenne announced victoriously, her hair tied in a messy knot on the top of her head and a pitchfork in her hand.

"You sure do."

Cheyenne shook her head and laughed.

This had been his dream, to marry Cheyenne and build a life together, working side by side during the day and making love at night. His dreams were simple. Cheyenne's were bigger. Cut and Shoot was too small. Even Texas wasn't big enough for her dreams. A bitter sadness spread across his chest.

"Come on, Cowboy. I'm hungry." They walked toward the gate where her car was parked. She clicked the lock. They hadn't been in a car together since high school. He had always been the driver. This was different. It was not what Colt had ever imagined. Maybe it could work? Cheyenne in the driver's seat?

Cheyenne smiled, almost as if she could read his thoughts. She drove them back to the main house. "Wow, Colt. This place is amazing. I'm glad you bought Potter's. It needed a good owner." There was an edge to her voice he didn't understand.

"Thanks. I've done all right." Colt helped her down from the cab of the truck.

"You've done more than all right. How did this happen, when I left, you—"

"Didn't have a pot to piss in or a window to throw it out of," he offered for her.

Cheyenne smiled. "I was going to say you were still working away for Old Man Potter. But you put it so much more eloquently. If I ever need a lyricist, I am calling you. But, seriously, how did you afford to buy Potter's ranch?"

"After you left, I threw myself into work. I did nothing but work, drink, and screw." Cheyenne winced at his words. Why? They'd both moved on. They both had a past. They were each other's first, but there was a lot after that for both of them; he was sure of it. "Anyway, this place was run into the ground. It went into foreclosure, and through sheer dumb luck, I had just enough to buy it, complete with four hundred head of cattle. I built it up from there."

"It's not luck, Colt. You were always the most driven person I know. Nobody works as hard as you."

He smiled at the praise.

"Why the new name? What does Night Latch mean?"

Colt hesitated before he told her. "Night Latch is the part you put on the saddle to give you something to hold on to when your horse tries to buck you off and break free. It's for the wildest horses. You know the type." He named it for her. He always wondered what would have been enough to keep her, but he would never tell her that.

"Ooh, who are you?" Cheyenne cooed as she bent down to pet his dog's head. The collie rubbed its head against her and wagged his tail, preventing them from going into the house. "You're gorgeous. What's your name?"

"That's Jasper. He couldn't work today. Had a sore paw, but looks like he is fine now. You'll be back out again with me tomorrow, right, boy?" Colt bent down and gave the dog a scratch behind the ears.

"You named him Jasper? Like the egg baby we had to raise together in seventh grade. Remember that? You did such a good job. I was always forgetting about it and leaving it in my locker. But you remembered."

Colt didn't answer. "Come on, boy."

"Wow," she said again when she walked into the entry hall. He looked at his house through her eyes, all ten thousand square feet of it. The front of the house was a wall of massive windows that overlooked the plains. "I'm glad I was never here before. I'm glad it's yours now." Her eyes clouded over as her thoughts drifted away.

"You never came here? Not even as a kid. Ron used to have the wildest parties. If he wasn't a State Trooper, he would have gotten himself in a lot more trouble." Colt laughed. Ron Potter was like a brother to him. Ron was five years older and five times wilder. He always lived a life close to the edge. "Have you seen him since you've been back?"

The color drained from Cheyenne's face. "No, um, no. I am just here to clear out my parents' house and play the gig in Houston."

Colt nodded. "I saw the video from the hospital. The one with you singing to the little girl from the *Broken* album."

She frowned. "You saw that too?"

"Darlin', everyone in the country saw that. It was nice of you to do that for her. You can tell she loved it. Sneaky girl, everyone knows you never sing songs from *Broken*."

"Yeah. But I couldn't say no. Not to her."

"Is she the reason you're doing the charity concert?"

Cheyenne glanced down at the floor. "Her parents contacted me a few months ago. They can't find a match. It's just so sad." The words caught in her throat.

"They will. Everyone in Texas is now registered. You did a good thing, Cheyenne. I'm proud of you."

Cheyenne wiped her eyes with the back of her hands. "You promised me food, Cowboy. Lead me to the kitchen."

"Words I've waited too long to hear. Cheyenne Ford wants to cook in my house." Colt grabbed her hand and led her through the hallway into the large room. It was bright. Had all the latest appliances. Colt had a problem of night-time purchases, which meant he had the best of all electronics.

Cheyenne laughed. "I bet."

Colt opened up the refrigerator that looked like a cabinet and pulled out as many vegetables as he could find and placed them on the counter.

"This ought to be a good start." Colt tapped the counter. His words were about the dinner, but he knew the depth of his sentence meant something more.

Cheyenne nodded and went to work. She washed and chopped the vegetables for a salad and made a sandwich while Colt fried a steak. "You sure you don't want one," Colt offered.

"Nope, the smell is good enough. But let's be honest, I might want to kiss you later, so I will taste it then anyway."

"Or I can make you your own. I'll still be kissing you

later. Don't worry about that, darlin'.''

Cheyenne laughed. "Nope, iron will."

"Yes, I experienced some of that iron will in the barn."

"Nope. That's different. You're my vice, Cowboy. Everyone needs at least one."

Colt sat down at the table beside her and held up his beer bottle to toast her. "To vices."

"To vices." She clinked her bottle against his. "You know what would be fun, to go for a ride. I don't get to the stables enough. J ... um, I don't have anyone to go riding with."

"Darlin', I spend all day in the saddle."

Cheyenne wrinkled her nose. "I suppose it stops being fun when it's your job."

"That's what every chef in the world says about food. Not that I would know," he added quickly. "I've never had a private chef."

Cheyenne laughed again. "Cowboy, they would have to pay you to cook in this kitchen. Are you on some sort of 'appliance of the month' plan?" She gestured to her surroundings. "I've never seen so many high-tech things in one place."

Colt tilted his head. "Well, that might be one of my vices."

"What? Appliances?"

Colt laughed. Unreal, it felt good to sit with her again. They used to talk for hours about everything. Then they would go riding. Cheyenne loved to ride. She said it cleared her mind. "I'll take you riding."

"Really?" Her eyes widened. "You will?"

Didn't she get it? He would do anything for her.

The sound of her phone cut the moment like a dull knife. It was out of place and didn't belong. Not in this moment. This was about them. "Shoot." Cheyenne sighed when she saw the number. "Hey," she said as she answered the phone. "No, yeah, I'm fine. I'm just ... um outside town ... Twenty minutes ... I'll be right, home ... No. No. I'm fine ... Really

… Okay, see you soon … Okay, me too."

Colt's hands clenched into fists. She was talking to Jamison. Fuck. It didn't matter if he was not wanting her for her body. He had something else that Colt wanted: her attention. All of it. He didn't want to share her attention with anyone, especially not another man. It didn't matter if he was gay or not.

Cheyenne put down the phone. "I need to go. Thanks—"

"For licking your pussy? Don't mention it." He sat back and took a swig of beer.

"Colt. Don't. Don't be like this again."

Colt stood up, his chair falling back as he rose. He couldn't do this. She wasn't ever going to be his. And he didn't need to get his hopes up with pretend nonsense. She had to go.

Cheyenne's mouth dropped as her eyes filled with tears. She shook her head and left.

CHAPTER TEN

Case Clayburn dropped the syringe into a portable medical waste bin. It helped Colt considerably that the only vet in Cut and Shoot happened to be his oldest brother. Case had gone to school at Texas A&M, but he chose to come home to set up his practice. It made sense. This was cattle country; there would always be a call for his services.

"He'll be fine. The antibiotics will take care of any infection."

Colt nodded as he ran a hand over the bull. The old boy had paid for half the ranch. God only knew how many cattle he had sired at this point—$150,000 a year worth, whatever that worked out to. Most meat in Texas could be traced back to him.

"Thanks, Case. I appreciate you coming out."

"Mama would have sent me anyway to check on you. You missed lunch on Sunday."

Colt didn't respond.

"This wouldn't have anything to do with Cheyenne being back in town?"

Colt pulled himself back into the saddle. He had work to do. "Thanks again, Case. Tell Mama I'll call her."

"You have been a right jackass since Cheyenne came

back to town. If you want to pretend that's not the case, you best change your attitude." Case tapped the syringe in his hand.

"I'm always a jackass. That's just me."

Case shook his head. He had the same black hair as Colt, but Cases' eyes were a blue-gray. "No, you're pigheaded at the best of times, but you're never mean. You've been an asshole since she stepped off her tour bus."

"She didn't bring her tour bus."

Case smiled. "I know. I was testing you."

"Why?" Colt stared at his brother. Why did Case always know how to get to him?

"Because if I asked if you had seen her, you wouldn't tell me on account of you being a jackass."

Colt sighed. "Yes. I've seen her."

"And."

"And what do you think? You just got done telling me what a piss poor mood I've been in. How do you think it went, Case? You're the smart one. How do you think it worked out for me?" Colt's chin jutted up at Case.

"So, you didn't talk to her?"

"Nope. The talking has been on the lighter side." Colt couldn't help but smile.

"What does that mean? You've seen her but not spoken. Like she won't speak to you. That's not like Cheyenne. "

"Case, you're far too interested in my sex life. It's time we got you someone." Colt tapped his brother's shoulder.

Case laughed. "Your sex life! You've had sex with Cheyenne Ford again. Man, I knew you would never get over her. That was fast work, even for you." He laughed again.

Colt ran a hand through his hair. Case always could get him to admit things he didn't want to. The talent was the bane of his childhood. Good to see he still had the annoying skill as an adult. "I'm not having this conversation with you. Thanks again for your help."

"Man, you don't have to talk, but you need to listen. You

have it bad for Cheyenne. You always have. Don't fuck it up. Don't let your pride get in the way."

"It's not my pride." Colt took off his hat and wiped the sweat from his brow. "Hell, maybe it is. Part of it. She left and just took off. Would not return my calls. Wouldn't see me. She just cut me off, like a switch had been tripped. It was over that quickly. We can't go back. I can't forgive her for that." Colt pressed his lips together. There was still so much anger inside him. Maybe it wasn't all anger. Maybe it was more like pain, but he couldn't express himself that way. It just wasn't in him. That was not who he was. The sensitive type. Nope.

"Yep. Cheyenne did a shitty thing. A decade ago. Move on. She was a kid. Are you going to let a mistake she made eleven years ago determine your happiness? That is some grudge you're nursing."

Colt couldn't believe he was having this conversation with his brother, the man who refused to discuss his private life with anyone. Chase shut those conversations down hard. Colt got it. Or he suspected, but Case had never confided in him. It hurt because they were close, but Case still didn't feel comfortable discussing his sexuality with anyone. Colt had never asked his other brothers if Case had confined in them, but he would know it if they had. The Clayburn brothers were tight; you only had to tell one for them all to know. So if Case had come out to Cord or Cane, Colt would have known all about it.

Yes, Texas was a red state, as conservative as they came, but Colt didn't give a shit about any of that. He wanted Case to be happy, to have someone. He was a great guy; he deserved to be happy. If a man made him happy, then Colt would be the first one to tell him to go for it. Life was too fucking short to care what other people thought.

"It's complicated with Cheyenne," Colt said finally. "I can't get past what she did. Maybe if I were a better man. But no, actually, if I were a better man, I would not be sniffing around her in the first place. She has moved on."

Colt put his hat back on.

"What does that mean? Is she married? Because I have a subscription to *PEOPLE* magazine at my office, and I'm sure that shit would have been on the cover. So what you mean is she is having sex with somebody else? Is that the problem, that she has had sex with other men?" Case glared at his brother.

"Shit, no. I don't care about that. I mean, I don't ever want to think about her being with anybody else, but no …" Colt ran his fingers along the brim of his hat. Might be time for a new one. The trim had a little fray on it.

"That's good to hear because I would have to deck you if you said that was the problem. You have slept with half the women in the state since she left. I lived through 'Colt Clayburn the manwhore' years. There were a couple of times I thought it was you I was going to need to give a shot of penicillin in the ass."

Colt shook his head and laughed. "I wasn't that bad."

"You were."

"Yeah, I was," Colt agreed. "But I always used condoms. No penicillin required."

"So what is the problem," Case pressed. "If she is not married, she is on the market. If you want her, go for it. Stake your claim and get over yourself. It has been more than ten years. Deal with it."

Colt let out a stream of air. Case was the smart one. "You're right. I'll call her. Maybe. Shit, I don't know. It's not the same. I don't know that I'll ever be what I was to her before."

"Of course not, a lot of time has passed. I doubt she thinks getting her a Pepsi and a handful of bluebonnets is the grand romantic gesture it was when you were kids. You're older, things have changed, you've changed." Case shrugged.

"That's the thing. We've changed. We don't work anymore. Together, I mean."

Case shot him a dubious glance. "You mean sexually."

"No! Hell no, that's fine. That part is great. That part was always going to be great. I mean, Christ, it is Cheyenne, it is going to be amazing." He took in a deep breath and pushed the memory of the barn to the back of his mind to be replayed later when he was alone. "That part is great. It's everything else that is shit. We can't talk anymore. Every time we do, I end up saying something—"

"Because you're being an asshole," Case finished the sentence for him.

"That pretty much sums it up."

"Well, stop. Stop being an asshole. Stop being butthurt for something she did so long ago."

"Because it's that easy?" Colt was tempted to tell him that it was easy to advise about women when you have never had a relationship with one, but his brother wasn't ready to go there yet. Soon, hopefully, because Case wasn't getting any younger. Nor was Colt, come to think about it. "Fine. I might call her." Calling was a good idea; he could not keep his hands off her when they were together. At least on the phone, they had a fighting chance at a meaningful conversation.

"Or you can talk to her at the concert tomorrow."

"Nah, I don't think so." Colt was unconvinced. Jamison would be there, and Colt would have to punch him. He just would. Why the hell did Cheyenne keep going back to him? Like Jamison was her best friend but more. It killed Colt. He wanted to be the number one in her life. And not just a hit album.

"Come on. You might not want to talk to her, but I do. Let's do it." Case's face lit up like they were kids on a chase for a wild rabbit. Except this wild rabbit was never going to be tamed. He was sure of it.

CHAPTER ELEVEN

Endless Supply (Back in the Saddle)

I'm sorry about your shirt
You know I'm lost in the dirt
Without you in my life

Baby, I'll buy another
Baby, there is no other
I just need you and your soft soft shirt

You wrap me in your arms
You wrap me in your soul
Our comfort level is like gold

The scent of your skin
It pulls me forever in
I just need you and your soft, soft shirt

I'm a fool
You play everything so cool
Baby, you brighten the worst of days

Baby, I'll buy another
Baby, there is no other
I just need you and your soft, soft shirt

Cheyenne pulled out her notebook and jotted down a few lines on the page. She had already written four new songs in the past two days. Passion can do that to a person. Especially an artist who might have crossed over a line that tugs on your heart and plays a chord in your soul. *Play me, baby.* Cheyenne wrote the words down. God, he knew how to play her. From her lips down to her fingertips. To sensations that rocked underneath her skin for days. Damn. He was good.

A studio trip was not scheduled for this visit, but when the melody dances within her veins, it's got to be played before it's gone. That's the way it had always worked for Cheyenne. Which meant she had to get in a last-minute spot at a music studio. For most people who requested a day of recording slot, it would be answered with a good solid laugh. But when your name is Cheyenne Ford, then spots open for you. As it did today. The Texas Get Registered Concert was set for six p.m. This gave Cheyenne a few hours of recording time. If need be, she could leave the studio and head straight to the concert.

She glanced over at Jamison. His brow was a little furrowed. "J, what's wrong? You're not worried about the concert, are you?"

Jamison glanced over in her direction. "I'm worried about you." His hands were gripped tight against the steering wheel. He never gripped the wheel like this.

"I added the extra security as you requested." She tapped her pen on the notebook.

Jamison parked the Escalade in front of the tall, red-bricked building. He grabbed her hand and traced his fingers over her wrists. "This is not okay."

Cheyenne's face heated. She tried to retract her hand. "It's not a big deal."

"Cheyenne, no woman should ever be marked. You are not one of his cows." Jamison grunted. His anger was at a level Cheyenne was not used to. Not from him.

She picked up her purse from the floor and opened the door. This was a discussion she did not want to have. Jamison was right; a woman shouldn't be marked, but that's not why she had the red marks on her wrists. That wasn't from an attempt to inflict pain. That was about pleasure. Colt would never try to intentionally hurt Cheyenne. At least not physically.

They walked in through the glass double door and to the reception spot. "Hi, I'm Cheyenne Ford."

"Yes, we're so excited to have you here, Ms. Ford. Right this way."

Cheyenne and Jamison followed behind the tall blond woman. She might have been a runway model back in the day. She had the height for it. Her pace was fast, almost like a run. What was the rush? They swerved through two different corridors before she opened a blue door with a guitar image drawn near the handle.

"Here you go." She waved them into the room. Cheyenne went into the studio while Jamison stayed back with all the sound machines. Blue, red, and green lights flashed throughout the room. This was her comfort zone. So much possibility could come from being here. Songs were words strung together, but the underlying melody always meant something more for Cheyenne. There was always a reason for her music. Each chord, each note, was a deliverance of emotion or memory, and Cheyenne was ready to get some of these out of her system. Colt had played too many tunes in her mind the last few days, and it was time to release some of them in the studio.

Cheyenne stroked the strings on her guitar. The first song she intended to record was one she only wanted to keep for herself. It was one of those get-it-out-now-or-forget-forever tunes, but she did not want this one gifted to the music world. *Ever.* This one was just for her ... and him, if they ever managed to see each other again. Colt had been a jerk again as she left. Kicked her out. Where was the polite cowboy she once knew?

The red rings on her wrists stared up at her like a forced memory. Yes, she remembered. She was there. Cheyenne didn't need to see the marks to remember. Her insides were still on fire days later from that moment in the barn. Colt had wanted to press into her the idea that she shouldn't have left. Was he as heartbroken as she had been? Did he care the same way she had? They were both so young. He never tried to come after her. Not that he would have been successful, but still, an attempt to reach out would have been nice. And now, all these years later, it's like they can't seem to get a break or to break away from each other. She could not stop the thoughts of him ... his smile ... his mouth ... his arms. Good lord, the man was a constant in her mind.

Cheyenne finished the song and took out her phone to text Colt before she could talk herself out of it.

I found this number in a bathroom stall. Said to text for a good time.

Thirty seconds later came the reply, *Wrong number.*

Cheyenne jerked her head back. That was quick. Less than a minute and he had already tried to shut her down. Good thing Cheyenne was not one to give up so easily. Especially not if it meant she could rile Colt's feathers. And if anyone's feathers needed to be rifled, they were Colt's. Cheyenne did not take kindly to being kicked out of his house. If she didn't have a tug on her heart, she would say forget the idea of forever with him. But something deep inside whispered for her not to give up. To try. What would a small attempt hurt?

Not possible. I was told this number hadn't changed in eleven years.

Colt replied, *Where are you?*

In the studio ... I've been inspired to write a new song.

After several minutes, Cheyenne placed her phone back

in her purse. She wasn't desperate. She was not going to send another text. No. If he was interested, he would respond. And if he didn't … well, then they were right back where they were before the text. Nowhere. A destination that had been marked on the map. Cheyenne and Colt's heartbreak drop-off. A place where Cheyenne could send off all her hopes and slightest ideas that maybe, just maybe they could have a go at things again. Granted, there was a lot of history and a lot of things that needed to be said. But just what if? What if they could be something again? That idea crushed her heart. She hadn't considered that idea in eleven years. Real love.

Cheyenne went back to her songs and made sure she got all the new material recorded. It was ten after two. They still needed to eat and change. She made her way out of the studio and gave instructions on how and where to send the music file.

Jamison eyed Cheyenne. His face hadn't softened from earlier. "Did you hear my new song? The one I wrote for you?" She poked his side. He didn't move. His eyes were dark.

"Cheyenne, I don't care about the shirt, but I do care about yours, and you came home with blood on it yesterday."

Cheyenne jerked her head back. Had she? Had there been blood on her shirt? That's right, Colt had a cut on his stomach.

"It was an accident, and it wasn't my blood."

The vein in Jamison's throat flexed. "That doesn't make it any better."

She wrapped her arms around his waist and kissed his cheek. "I love you, J."

The sides of his mouth pulled up. "I love you too, princess."

***

"Yea, baby, that's right … Right there. Do it. Say it."

Cheyenne stopped in the hallway backstage. The door next to her dressing room was slightly cracked open. Through the sliver was an image of Delilah Grant with her skirt pushed up over her hips and some guy on his knees in front of her exposed thighs.

Cheyenne gasped and motioned for Jamison to give her a minute. Delilah needed to be on stage to open in less than five minutes. Oh, Dear Lord, Cheyenne did not need to deal with this right now. Delilah was relatively new on the scene, but she had already established a reputation for intense behind-the-scenes behavior. More than one person had tried to dissuade Cheyenne from asking Delilah to open for her on her last tour, but Cheyenne saw beyond Delilah's antics.

Even underneath her heavy stage makeup, there was a flash of the insecure young woman that Delilah tried to hide. Beneath her purple and black sheered wig, there was a head full of golden-brown hair and a sweet-natured woman. Cheyenne saw someone that needed some support. Someone she could trust. This industry was tough, being that young, and her vice was not helpful for her heart. Cheyenne wanted to lend some warmth to the coldness that Delilah surrounded herself with. She had liked Delilah from day one, not just her spitfire, gritty songs, but more so the sultry soft ones. Delilah wasn't just an unpolished star, she was a visionary of music, and Cheyenne loved being on tour with her.

But her backstage antics were going to get her in trouble. The girl needed some heavy hands to reel her back in. Country music is not the place for tawdry behavior from a lady; despite the double standard, it was what it was.

"You're not a country darling," the man on his knees repeated.

"That's right, and don't you forget it." Delilah pushed her skirt down and walked toward the door.

Cheyenne gave Delilah a minute to get herself together

before she entered her dressing room.

"Hey, Cheyenne, I was just about to go out. Is everything all right?"

Cheyenne took a deep breath. She didn't want to lecture Delilah or make her feel judged, because Cheyenne was the last person to judge anybody for their private life, but Cheyenne had an overwhelming need to protect Delilah because someone needed to look after her. "Yes, sweetie, listen, it's none of my business what happens in your room, but you've got to be mindful and at least close the door. Too many busybodies are lurking these halls hoping to give a tell-all." There was more she could say, but it would have to wait until after the show.

"I'll be more careful." Delilah let out a soft giggle and made her way to the stage.

Jamison led Cheyenne backstage and stood outside her door while she got dressed. Though it wouldn't matter if he was inside the room, he had seen her naked plenty of times. Cheyenne brushed the bronzer over her cheeks. God, she hoped they would find a donor today. That would make all of it, all of this worth it. Even the heartbreak of seeing a glimmer of Colt slide by would still be worth it if they could get a donor. One match, that's all they needed. She ran the lip gloss over her mouth and stood. Her light turquoise dress was almost sheer. The fabric swayed as she walked. She had shown it to Jenn before Cheyenne left the hospital, told Jenn that she was wearing it to match the stud earrings in Jenn's ears. Cheyenne's shoes were a light sliver with little sparkles of glitter along with the ribbons that tied over her ankles.

As she looked at herself in the mirror, a knock on the door made her jump. "Hey, you ready?" Jamison took in a deep breath. "You look gorgeous, better than ever. Jenn will be excited."

"Thank you. Will you take my picture? So I can send it to her?" Cheyenne handed him the phone.

"Yes, and one for me too." He winked at her and snapped a few photos on her phone, then one on his own.

"Jamison, I want you to watch out for Delilah. She might seem like she is hardcore, but that girl is covering up something more than her hair."

Jamison let out a laugh. "Yes, she reminds me a bit of someone else I met several years ago."

Cheyenne gave him a shove. "Not even."

He grabbed her hand and kissed it. "Cheyenne, you were hurting. You did a lot of things to act out. Remember the Boiler Room escapade?"

She groaned. "Never mention that."

He smiled. "I won't, and I'll keep my eyes on Delilah when they aren't on you."

"Which is never." She laughed as Jamison led her out to the stage, then leaned back and kissed his cheek once they arrived.

He patted her behind. "Make me proud, princess." The sides of his mouth pulled up. He was a sexy, beautiful man.

"Did they find a match? The organizer said all the typing should be done by now so I could announce they had found a match on stage."

Jamison squeezed the bridge of his nose between his thumb and his forefinger. "They're still going over the numbers. Just deliver a Cheyenne-worthy performance; we'll deal with everything else later."

"Y'all know I'm not your country darlin', but I couldn't be prouder to be here today with the one and only Cheyenne Ford. Y'all give it up for country music's one and only country darlin'." Delilah clapped her ring-covered hands above her head.

Cheyenne walked out on stage. The arena was packed. She scanned the crowd as if she could identify the match by sight. Hope and everything else had been put into this concert. There had to be a match out there. Someone in this crowd could be the donor for Jenn. Tonight, Cheyenne would sing for that person. Lights flashed at her as people snapped photos on their cell phones.

Cheyenne waved to the crowd before she grabbed the microphone. "Hey, y'all, thanks for coming out today and supporting this great cause and getting registered." She glanced down for a second. "This is a charity I hold dear to my heart."

With a stroke of her guitar, she belted out "Back in the Saddle." The crowd sang along with her and cheered for more. Cheyenne continued to sing. She was here to give them a good concert, and that she would. Cheyenne loved to sing, and even better, to perform—it was her wheelhouse. She was comfortable on stage, as comfortable as she would be with her head on a blanket of bluebonnets and her eyes on the clouds. This was happiness.

A sliver of worry shot through her despite the flow of serotonin that warmed her skin from being on stage. If only they could find a match. Then Cheyenne could imagine the dream of a wooden-paneled ranch home with a beachside view, as if that were even possible. But hopefully, this was. It had to be. A donor was out there. Cheyenne knew this with every inch of her soul. There was going to be a match for Jenn.

She glanced at Jamison. His eyes were a lighter shade of green. She had seen this shade before. Once. When his mom passed away. A lump caught in her throat. Cheyenne knew why he was sad. There was no match. That is why he brushed off the question. He would never lie to her, so he didn't directly answer the question.

Cheyenne kept singing. Her heart could break after this set, and it would. Unlike every concert she had ever played, Cheyenne did not lose herself in the music. She was conscious of every note, every face, every flash of light from the audience. She had failed. The only reason for coming home was to find a match. Why couldn't she make this happen? There had to be a match. It didn't make sense. With all those registrations, surely one of them would work?

Finally, it was over. Every song on the list was

performed. "Thank you. Thank you." Cheyenne waved and made her way off the stage. She might have fallen if it weren't for Jamison and his strong arms wrapped underneath her. He pulled her in close and kissed her head before tipping her head up. "It's just the numbers here. We'll keep looking."

The whole point of the concert was to find a donor. A match. Cheyenne wanted nothing less than to perform at this point, and she had one more song to go. That was the deal she had made with the stadium, an eight-song set, and then an encore. Nine songs. Eight songs down and one to go. One song more and she could leave. Every bit of pain tugged inside. She didn't want to put on her signature smile and entertain a crowd. She wanted to run and get away as far as possible from this moment.

Jamison wiped the tear from underneath her eye.

Cheyenne met his gaze. "The quicker we get out of here the better. This town is filled with nothing but heartache."

"Go break some hearts with a good song." Jamison squeezed her shoulders.

Cheyenne forced a smile and made her way back on stage. "Thank you for that applause. Wow, Texas does know how to do it big!" She managed a giggle.

Shouts came from the audience, "Play from *Broken*! Play 'Sunset on Us'! *Broken*"! Cheyenne smiled. It was a skill she had acquired in this business, always be ready to smile. If you're on stage, so is your smile.

"Y'all, I thank you for loving me and loving *Broken*—I just can't."

Awes passed through the crowd.

"I tell you what. How about I play a new song for you? This will be the first time anyone has ever heard it."

The crowd cheered louder than they had before with any of her other songs, and those had been great. But this was different. She had offered an exclusive first listen. Anyone and everyone would be thrilled to say they had heard a first-time song from Cheyenne Ford. She could do this. This was a song she could belt out and get into.

Cheyenne let the first chord of her guitar go and caught Jamison's eye. She gave him *the* look. It was their look. One they shared exclusively. He nodded. He would get her through this. He got her through everything.

"This one is called 'Endless Supply.' It is for the man in my life who always has my back and manages to make me smile when nobody else can. This one is for you, J."

Cheyenne sang the song for Jamison, and the crowd swayed along to the beat. This would be a hit. The energy in the room was enough of a confirmation. The song was going gold, but that didn't matter. Nothing mattered without a match for Jenn.

As Cheyenne hit the final note on "Endless Supply," a tall, dark, and handsome cowboy had appeared from the side of the stage. She let her fingers strum the last chords on her guitar as her eyes met the crowd, and she winked. "Thank you, everyone, for coming out today and for getting registered." She waved to the crowd and blew her double kiss as she exited the stage and into Colt's arms. "You came." She kissed his cheek. He was here. She wasn't sure he would after the way things had ended last time. Colt was obviously mad about her departure, but that was without any information. There was still more that needed to be said. But she wasn't ready. That discussion was going to take a lot of courage, and she wasn't sure if it would result in any type of possibility for a future. It was the fear of the unknown that wrangled inside her mind. On most days it was too much for her. How could she think Colt would ever be able to swallow her truth?

Cheyenne eyed Colt. They used to share everything. All their secrets and dreams. Now, they were like strangers. Neither one of them seemed to budge.

"Yeah, and now I'm leaving." There was no warmth coming from him.

"Why?" She took a step backward.

"I came here to lay down a claim to you and us, but

you're up there on stage singing songs about him?" He took off his hat and ran his hands through his dark hair. It seemed darker now. Most likely from the anger that radiated off from him. Why was he so upset?

"It's just a song. I—"

"No, Cheyenne, it's not just a song. And I'm not going to be your second-hand man. We're done. For good this time."

Anger flashed in her. "You know what, you're right. It's not just a song. What I have with Jamison goes way back. He's been there for me. He was there for me when you weren't."

"When I wasn't? When wasn't I there for you? When you slammed your truck door in my face and kicked up the dust as you drove out of town?" He shoved his hat back on his head.

"It wasn't like that. I had to go. You wouldn't have understood." Cheyenne eyed the floor. This was not the place for this conversation. Not here. Not now. Not ever, even though she knew better. It was going to have to happen at some point. Just not right now. They needed privacy for that. All the ears and cameras that were within reach should not be privy to that discussion.

"Maybe, but it's not like you gave me a chance. Or us. I guess all you care about is yourself."

Jamison approached Cheyenne from behind and shook his head.

Both Cheyenne and Colt's attention went to Jamison. Shoot. She should not argue with Colt about Jamison in front of Jamison. It sure would make matters more difficult.

Jamison's chest muscles were tight as the vein in his jaw flexed in solid, steady motions as he waited for a response from Cheyenne.

"You should leave and stay far away from her." Jamison's green eyes had darkened to an almost indeterminable shade. Fury swirled around his body. His hands were clenched into fists that most likely wanted to release their rage onto Colt.

It was Colt's turn to laugh. "What's this now? Are you telling me to stay away from Cheyenne? Huh … that's really funny. You must not be that close."

"All right, to the parking lot." Jamison poked Colt's chest.

"J, don't do it. It's not worth it." Cheyenne grabbed on to his bicep.

"Stay here." Jamison's eyes warned as he followed behind Colt.

There was no way she was going to stay. She scanned the backstage crew and another dark-haired guy caught her eye. Case Clayburn. Colt's older brother was here. She had not seen him in years. God, she loved him. He had been like a brother to her too, until she left. She rushed up to his side and grabbed his arm. "Case, hurry. Colt is about to get in a fight."

"What? It's been forever since he's fought anyone." He tipped his hat to her. "Great show by the way. It's so nice having you back in Texas." He squeezed her in tight. Pleasantries couldn't be missed around Case. He was the town veterinarian and a hot commodity; he always had been. Cheyenne was sure that single girls from a hundred miles away had tried to rope him in.

Rain began to pour as they hit the parking lot. Buckets of water soaked the men and the crowd that had formed. The night lit up as lightning split the sky. Colt and Jamison stood a couple of feet apart, both nostrils flared. Their eyes were filled with anger. Their shirts clung to their chests like muscular armor. They were evenly matched. This would be a difficult battle that would not be easily won.

A swarm of photographers clicked away as their flashes mimicked the sky full of bolts of lightning. No. This shouldn't happen. Pain tore at Cheyenne's insides.

"I suppose I'll let you take the first swing since I've been taking my swings at your—"

Jamison's right fist clocked across Colt's jaw before he

got the last word out. Jamison didn't need to be asked twice. Colt took a step back before he took an uppercut to Jamison's jaw. A pound came across Colt's face. Jamison's solid knuckles hit him again. Rain poured down on the crowd, but no one dispersed. Everyone wanted to see this fight and what was behind it.

"Stay away from her. I haven't seen Cheyenne cry this much in a decade, and she's only been back here less than a week." Jamison swung at Colt and hit him in the stomach.

Colt buckled for a second and took a hard clock to Jamison's face. "At least she is feeling some emotion. All that pent-up frustration from years of bad sex with you cock-blocking everyone in her vicinity, I suppose."

"I wouldn't call good sex ripped shirts and blood-stained clothes, and don't even get me started on her wrists." He lunged for Colt and took him down to the ground.

Cheyenne tapped Case. "You have to do something."

Case forced himself between the two men. "Stop. Colt. Stop this right now." He pulled Colt off the ground.
"Move out of the way, Case, I'm about to finish him." Colt wiped the blood from his lip.

"Finish me? I'm just getting started." Jamison took another swing, but Case jumped in between the shot and received the hard blow, falling to the ground. Both Jamison and Colt knelt next to Case and shook him.

Cheyenne dropped to her knees and leaned over Case's body. "Case, are you okay?" Blood trickled from a split above his brow.

"Oh, hey, Cheyenne. Did Colt finally get through to you?"

She scrunched her eyebrows. "Does it hurt bad?" She ran her hand over his cheek.

"Good. I'm okay. I'm glad you're back. Colt is a real ass without you around." He sat up.

"I'm sorry for hitting you." Jamison offered his hand to help Case up.

"Thanks. No worries. It wasn't the first hit, and I'm sure

it won't be the last one I'll be taking for my brother."

Colt's eyes were on Cheyenne, who was filled with tears. She should have stopped this, but everything happened too fast, and now people were injured. Her eyes couldn't be brought up to glance at Colt's. Too much had been said, not enough had been explained, and it was all her fault. The rain washed over her body and all possibilities of any kind of future with Colt. She ruined it. Again.

GIA STONE

CHAPTER TWELVE

Colt wiped the blood from his lip. A metallic taste filled his mouth. It was over. It had been over for over a decade. He finally got it.

Yet, why the hell had she texted him to say she had written a new song when it was about Jamison? Why would she think he wanted to know about that? Was that her way of getting back at him for what he said after the barn? Of all the fucked-up ways to end it with someone …

He looked over at his brother. Case's eye was already starting to swell. Ah, shit. "Man, that is going to need some ice."

"You didn't fare much better. Still have all your teeth?"

Colt grunted his response. His teeth were fine, but pride had taken a beating. Cheyenne only wanted him for one thing. She'd called Jamison the only man in her life who had her back. Unbelievable.

Case put his hand around Colt's shoulders. "If it makes you feel any better, that guy looks a whole lot worse than you. You got him pretty good. His face is pretty mangled. Wouldn't be surprised if you broke one of his ribs. That was a good shot."

Colt shook his head. "Nope. It doesn't make me feel any

better." And Colt knew it wasn't true. They might have fared the same. But it didn't matter.

"Sorry."

"Me too."

Colt was sorry for going down that route again. When he saw her being carried into the Broken Spoke, he should have kept driving. He knew better, and he still made the wrong decision. Just like showing up at her concert. All he could see was red. It was not from the blood. He was furious. He was mad at himself. But even madder at Cheyenne. She wasn't the sweet girl he grew up with. She was a cruel woman.

CHAPTER THIRTEEN

Put on Your Spurs

Hot Texas sun
You were always the one
Making me smile
Had you for a moment, but, baby, it's been a while

Saw you by the fence
Dripped in sweat
I couldn't look away

You roped me in with your sexy skin
And I can't seem to win
I can't back away

Cowboy, don't leave me
This time I want to stay

Lay me down in a bed of hay
Run your spur along me all day
Tie me up in your lies
Wrap me up in your rope

Baby, I'm in boot-deep

Warmed me with your metal
Warmed me with you your heart
Cowboy, this time is different
Cowboy, we can't part

Lay me down in a bed of hay
Run your spur along me all day
Tie me up in your lies
Wrap me up in your rope
Baby, I'm in boot-deep

"Do you want me to go in with you?" Jamison asked as he pulled into a parking spot in front of the Houston skyscraper. The street at ground level was always in the shadows because the colossal building prevented the sunlight from ever reaching the ground.

"No. I need to do this alone."

Cheyenne had told Jamison the story years ago through drunk tears as she hung on to the toilet. She had never intended on telling anyone. Jamison had held her hair as everything came out, including her secrets. He'd put her in the shower, got her cleaned up, and put her to bed. In the morning, he gave her an ultimatum, stop the benders or he would walk away. He couldn't watch her slowly killing herself with vodka. So, she did. She stopped drinking almost entirely. She had the odd glass of wine, but she never got blackout drunk anymore. Well, she stopped drinking hard until she got back to Cut and Shoot. She could not handle this town sober, and Jamison got that.

"I'll wait down here. Call if you need me." He handed her the phone. She almost forgot it. Her mind was focused on one thing.

Veritas Investigation was on the top floor. Cheyenne stepped into the office and took in the view. Windows lined the room. At this height, all of Downtown Houston could be seen. A panoramic display of the city showed the Bayou in the various shades of silver and blues that were pieced together by the large buildings.

A tall russet-haired woman greeted Cheyenne at the door. She was striking, with strong features and bright blue eyes. Her height and muscular frame gave her a commanding presence, like a cross between an Amazonian warrior and a Greek goddess. "Hi, Miss Ford. I'm Vanessa Lee. We spoke on the phone."

"Yes. Thanks for agreeing to meet with me. As I mentioned on the phone, discretion is paramount." Cheyenne took in a deep breath.

"Of course. Owen Hayes is the best. You came to the right place."

Cheyenne smiled. She had read about Veritas online; he was the best. This was something she prayed she would never have to do, confront her past, but it was no longer an option. She had been able to run from it for a long time, but it had caught up with her. Choices had been made, and now she would have to find out the truth. No longer could she take out her journal and pen and work through her troubles with a tune. A song wasn't going to fix this situation. At least the attempt of that was over. The concert did not work.

"Owen is in his office. You're in good hands." Vanessa laid her hand on Cheyenne's arms. Her warmth was the right temperature for this situation.

"Hi, I'm Owen Hayes." Owen greeted her at the door to his private office. He was younger than she expected. In her mind, a PI should be a middle-aged man with a dark past and a long list of vices. Every book she had read supported that hypothesis, but Owen only looked a few years older than her. He had sandy blond hair and a friendly smile. He was handsome if fair men were your thing.

Cheyenne spotted family photographs on his desk and immediately felt at ease.

"Is that your wife?" Cheyenne pointed to the picture of a woman on the beach cuddling two toddler boys. They both were the carbon copy of Owen.

"Yeah, that's my wife, Nine, and our boys, Garret and Johnny. You just missed them. She brings them in for lunch most days. We usually have a picnic in the park across the street."

Cheyenne smiled, even though her heart ached. Realization struck her. She wanted what she saw in the picture. She wanted a man that smiled when he said her name. She wanted a husband to meet for lunch and babies; she wanted babies.

Where had that come from? Cheyenne had a career she loved. She had Jamison. She had financial security. She had more happiness in her life than she was entitled to, but she wanted to smile like the woman in the photo. She brushed away the thought. "Nine? Cool name."

"Yeah, it is. She's great." Owen's lips curled into a smile at the sound of his wife's name.

That. That is what Cheyenne wanted; someone to smile when they thought about her. "How did you meet?"

Owen laughed. "Now there is a story. I was hired to investigate her."

Cheyenne's mouth dropped open before she quickly regained her composure and snapped it shut again.

"See, that is the exact look my wife gave me. It wasn't my finest hour, but it all worked out in the end."

"There is a song in there somewhere." Cheyenne smiled.

"You should write it. My wife is a big fan. We were at your concert last night."

"Oh, wow. I wish I would have known. I would have gotten you backstage passes."

"Next time."

Cheyenne sighed. She would not be playing in Houston again. That was a one-off, for the charity.

"You explained to Vanessa you need a DNA test done, is that right?"

Cheyenne took a deep breath. This was real. Not getting away from it now. She could not just record a song and forget about it this time. "Yes. But the man can't know. I don't know how you are going to get his DNA, but ..."

"I can get it. Don't worry about that. I have his name and social security and his home address." Owen looked down at the file. "The DNA sample won't be a problem."

"Okay." Cheyenne wanted to believe him.

"What we do from there is up to you." Owen's eyes lay a level of security one could only hope for.

Cheyenne took a deep breath. Everything was so real. Sometimes she was fooled into believing the song lyrics were just words, not her life, her story.

They spoke for a few minutes longer, and then Cheyenne left. Less than fifteen minutes is all it took.

"Hey, how did it go?" Jamison asked as he opened the passenger door.

"It's done." Those were the only words she could let fall from her mouth. She didn't want to talk to anyone right now, not even J.

They drove back in silence from Houston, listening to the radio until "This Isn't Goodbye" came on, and then she had to turn it off. Four albums, and of course that is the one the radio station chose to play today.

"I need a drink." Cheyenne noticed the *Welcome to Cut and Shoot* sign on the highway and immediately alcohol came to mind. "Take me to the bar, J. I might even dance with you."

A short drive later, Jamison steered the Escalade into the parking lot. "Cheyenne, do you want to do that to yourself again? I can drive us home tonight. You can sleep. We will be in Nashville when you wake up." Jamison pulled her body into his and ran his fingers through her hair. "You can recline your chair back and snuggle up with your purple blanket."

"No, I need a drink."

Jamison cocked his head to the side. It was almost as if he wanted to say something but didn't. "Princess, it's going to be okay. I promise." He breathed into her ear and wrapped his arm around her waist, then led her to the same stool she had sat on before.

"Hey, Nick, can I get a double Crown." She was here to drink, not joke.

"Sure thing, Cheyenne." Nick poured the caramel-colored liquid into a glass.

"Thanks, and please keep them coming." Cheyenne slammed back the drink. She wanted to knock out her sense of reality. All of the hopes that had danced in her head had now slipped through a dirty street gutter to disappear forever. Cheyenne didn't want to imagine that place. Her only possibility for peace was going to be if she flushed out this memory.

"Hey, Cheyenne, that was such a good concert!" The blond was back. She must be a regular, but then again, this was the only bar in town as far as Cheyenne knew.

"Thank you so much, I'm glad you enjoyed it." The sides of Cheyenne's mouth pulled up into a wide smile. The best she could force with the lack of whiskey not being fully pumped in her veins.

Nick returned with another round, and Cheyenne sipped it back. She wanted to forget but not fall out of her chair. Though she knew Jamison wouldn't let that happen. He would keep her safe no matter what. And she wouldn't do that to him again. She was in a bad place then.

The DJ came across the loudspeaker. "Hey, everyone, I've got a little special something for you. A new release from Cut and Shoot's country darling Cheyenne Ford."

Jamison raised an eyebrow at her. "You already released 'Endless Supply'?"

"No, I didn't release any of the songs. I just sent them in so I wouldn't forget them. I hadn't even had a chance to listen to them yet." She sipped on her drink. She did not want to hear whatever song was about to play.

The speaker was like a poison-filled dart that aimed directly to her heart. Bullseye. The first chord spilled through the room and split open a wound Cheyenne wanted to heal. She slammed her hands down on the bar. "Dammit."

She rushed to the bathroom and threw up in the stall. She sunk to her knees and wiped her mouth with the back of her hand.

No. No one was ever going to hear that song. That was *her* song. Their song if it had ever happened. Dammit. Someone was going to get fired for this. Or Someones. This was an invasion of her privacy, and she didn't take that lightly. Cheyenne needed to get out of this bar and this town. She should have listened to Jamison and let him drive her home and back to Nashville tonight.

Cheyenne rinsed out her mouth and wiped her face with a wet paper towel. She didn't let herself look at the wall, at the spot Colt had held her and … No. That was over, just another mistake to add to her list.

She made her way back to where Jamison sat. The dance floor was full. There were less than a thousand people in this town, but they were all here, a sea of denim and cowboy boots, dancing and swaying to the beat of a Luke Bryan song.

Jamison's eyes were on her. He always watched for her safety. He was her safety. Her special happy place. Cheyenne took in a deep breath. It would take strength, but she could move on. One foot in front of the other, that's all she needed to do.

Cheyenne gasped. The figure of a man she had hoped to never see again crossed in front of her line of sight. An evil man. He was larger now. He had been big back then, but now he seemed even bigger. Evil permeated around him. Even without a glance of his face. His energy was dark and made the hairs against Cheyenne's skin prick up. She froze. The man turned, and their faces met. Darkness overcame Cheyenne, and she slumped to the ground.

CHAPTER FOURTEEN

"Hey, Colt. Haven't seen you around in a while."

Colt smiled up from the barstool he was sitting at next to his brother. Desiree Mulsow smiled back at him. She had seen him around plenty, but that was the code for when they were both single. They were the other's port in a storm. Neither would be the other's first choice, but they screwed occasionally. She was pretty, some might find her beautiful, but not Colt.

"Things off again with Chris?" Colt guessed.

"I don't want to talk about him."

"So that is a yes." He really should tell her that if she wanted to make a go with Chris, she should stop screwing Colt every time they broke up.

"Dance with me," Desiree whined.

Colt shook his head. He was here to drink. Case had talked him into coming out and licking his wounds. Just as easy to be depressed in a bar, and more access to liquor, that was Case's argument for coming out. It seemed solid logic at the time.

"Dance with the lady." Case pushed Colt off the stool. If he hadn't had such a firm grip on his beer, he would have spilled it.

Colt shot his brother an angry look. "Looks like we're dancing." He put his bottle on the bar and followed Desiree to the dance floor. If he was going to get back on the horse, Desiree was as good as any.

Colt placed his hands on her hips and maneuvered her so he could watch Cheyenne over her shoulder. Of course she was here. Where wasn't she? He couldn't even sleep without her turning up. And it wasn't even a good dream, no replay of the barn for him. He dreamed of going to pick her up at a bus station, but she never gets off the bus. He spends the rest of the dream searching for her.

At the end of the song, the DJ came on, "Hey everyone, I've got a little special something for you. A new release from Cut and Shoot's country darling Cheyenne Ford."

Colt clenched his teeth until his jaw ached. He wasn't drunk enough to listen to another song Cheyenne had written for Jamison. God, he wished Case hadn't pulled him off. He needed to get in at least more three good punches before he could take his hate from a rolling boil to a low simmer.

Colt stopped moving when he heard the lyrics. "Cowboy, don't leave me. This time I want to stay." *What the hell?* She called Colt cowboy, not that asshole. "Warmed me with your metal, warmed me with your heart. Cowboy, this time is different. Cowboy, we can't part. Lay me down in a bed of hay. Run your spur along me all day." He shook his head. Cheyenne was singing about him. This song was written for *him*. What was she doing? He needed to speak to her. This was insane. Clearly, he meant something to her. Or maybe he didn't, but he needed to know one way or the other.

"Excuse me, Desiree, I need to go speak to someone. Go find Chris. You love him, he loves you. Stop messing about and settle down with him already. He is a good man."

Desiree scowled, not used to being told what to do.

Cheyenne had run into the bathroom when the song started, so he forced himself to wait for her on the dance floor. They needed to talk, not screw against the wall again.

When the music ended, Cheyenne returned to the bar. *It's now or never, Cowboy. Time to lay your claim. No more messing about.* That was good advice he gave. Now he just needed to take it.

As Cheyenne turned around, the color drained from her face. Her smile faltered, replaced by fear, sheer terror. He had only seen that look before in an animal in pain, confused and hurt. Colt's head snapped back to see who she was looking out for.

Ron Potter.

What? They were friends, had been since they were kids. Why would she be upset to see Ron?

Colt didn't have long to think about it as Jamison jumped out of his seat and crossed to Cheyenne. Colt couldn't hear what they said, but he saw Cheyenne nod and sway as she grabbed Jamison for support. She was going to pass out.

Colt immediately ran to her side. "Cheyenne," he cried out, reaching her just before her eyes rolled back. She collapsed into his arms.

"What the hell," Colt demanded.

"It was you," Jamison sneered at Ron. The veins in his neck pulsed with every beat of his heart. Hatred radiated off him. Colt had been on the receiving end of some of his blows, and he had not looked that angry then. This was different. This was rage, unbridled and fierce. "You mother fucker. It was you."

Jamison didn't give Ron a chance to respond. He swung at him, and Ron's head snapped back, blood instantly gushing from his nose. Shit, he had broken it. Jamison hit him again, this time in the gut, and then another blow to his eye. What the fuck was going on?

"Case!" Colt shouted for his brother, dragging him into another fight. Colt was going to hear about this later.

Case shook his head but still hopped off the stool to join Colt.

Jamison continued to pummel Ron before pulling him forcibly out into the parking lot. Fuck, Jamison was going to kill Ron. You don't move a fight unless shit is about to get real. "Case, stay with Cheyenne."

Colt ran into the parking lot. Jamison had Ron's gun. He'd taken it from Ron when he pulled Ron outside. For a second, Colt thought Jamison was going to shoot Ron, but he laid the gun behind him and lunged at Ron again, hitting him over and over in the face. Blood covered both men. "Admit it, you mother fucker, or I'm going to kill you," Jamison wailed as he pounded into Ron's face.

Jamison pulled the handcuffs from Ron's belt and shackled his hands together. "Doesn't feel good, does it, being handcuffed?" Jamison kicked him and shook his head; tears were in his eyes. "Asshole. How could you do that to her?" His voice broke as he began to cry.

"Is this about the letters? Those were a joke."

Jamison shook his head. "Of course those were from you, you worthless piece of shit. Such a fucking coward. You were then too. That's why you had to handcuff her, couldn't risk her fighting back."

Colt stood between the two men: one he hated, the other had been his friend since before he could remember.

Ron cocked his head to the side to wipe the blood from his face on his shoulder. "I don't know what you think you know. But you're wrong. She wanted it." Jamison lunged at him, but Colt prevented him from delivering another blow.

"Admit it," Jamison bellowed.

"She wanted it. She can't admit it now, but she wanted it. Nobody forced anybody."

Colt froze. Dread coiled in him. Who were they talking about? Terror shot through his spine as the answer stared him in the eye. *Fuck no.* Don't let it be Cheyenne. Oh god, but who else could it be? "Who are you talking about?" Colt asked. There was no emotion in his voice, no feeling at all. He was numb. They could not be talking about Cheyenne, his Cheyenne. No. It couldn't be her. "Who are you talking about?" he asked again. The words barely made it past his lips.

"Cheyenne," Jamison said when Ron didn't answer.

Colt slowly nodded. Puzzle pieces slid into place, answers to questions he did not know to ask.

"When?" Colt took in another breath to steady his nerves. "When," he asked again when no one answered.

"I'm sorry, man. I know we're friends. I shouldn't have done it. She came onto me. It was a long time ago."

Colt swallowed hard. Ron was the reason she left. "Take off the handcuffs," Colt said.

"No. Did you hear what he just said? He admitted it."

Colt shook his head. His best friend and his girlfriend. No. Fuck no. "He didn't admit anything. Take off the handcuffs."

Jamison did not move.

"Take off the fucking handcuffs!" Colt shouted. He took the keys from Ron's belt and undid them himself.

"I'm sorry, man," Ron said.

"Don't fucking apologize to me!" Colt roared, then swung at Ron and hit him square in the jaw. "You didn't rape me! You raped Cheyenne! No apology will replace what you took." Colt slammed his fists into Ron's face over and over. If Ron tried to fight back, he failed because the only impact Colt endured was his fists battering Ron's face. He pulled back to deliver a harder blow, but his arm was stuck. Someone was restraining him.

"Get off. Get the fuck off me," Colt sneered. He wasn't done.

Jamison continued to pull Colt back. "Cheyenne is watching you. Don't let her see you kill a man."

Somehow the words penetrated the enraged fog. His head snapped up. Cheyenne stood in the doorway, her face covered in tears and Case's arm was around her for support. Oh god, how long had she been there? Only then did Colt realize the camera phones were pointed at him. It had been captured on video, all of it. Of fuck. It would be on the internet before the blood dried. Cheyenne was upset about the video of her singing in the hospital being uploaded without her consent. What was this going to do to her? Shit, all her secrets were exposed for the titillation of the country.

Colt turned to Jamison. "Take her home." It went against every instinct to let Cheyenne go home with anyone else, but Jamison would keep her safe. Jamison protected her from Ron. He would protect her from this too. "I will stay with Ron until the police get here. Just take Cheyenne home. Take care of her, man." He was trusting him with her.

"I will. I always do."

CHAPTER FIFTEEN

Bathwater Full of Love (Back in the Saddle)

You washed away years of pain
Unspoken words filled with shame
A decade of regret
I was soaking wet

You took your sponge
And ran it over me
Giving me back my dignity

All those years and you're still the one
Filling up my tub with so much fun
In bathwater full of love

The day you arrived
I was ready to leave
You broke down my guard
It was almost too hard

You wouldn't let go
And I was down so low

You pulled away my layers
Now I'm exposed and bare

All those years and you're still the one
Filling up my tub with so much fun
In bathwater full of love

Cheyenne rushed into the house. Flashes of light flickered behind her as Jamison shut down the shades.

"I'll call Nashville and see if the news has hit there yet."

Cheyenne's shoulders slumped. "I may not be the brightest butterfly of social media, but I'm smart enough to know that the news has hit Nashville, or it will have by the time we arrive."

Jamison pulled her into his arms. He was sweaty and had blood on him from the fight.

She backed away. "You have to get rid of that shirt. It has his blood on it."

He tore it off his chest and threw it in the fireplace. "I'll burn it." True to his word, Jamison lit the fire. The flame lit a hard red and orange glare before it settled into a soft yellow glow.

"I'm going to take a shower. Don't go near the windows, and don't open the door."

"I won't." She wanted to let him embrace her again, but he had to be clean first. The idea of Ron's scent or blood near her own was too much to take. She swallowed hard and sunk into the couch.

A voice warned her not to. But she couldn't help herself. She found her phone in her purse and pulled up Twitter. There it was, her name all over again. This time it was worse. It wasn't a sweet hospital song. It was her horrible, buried past that had surfaced for all to see and hear. It wasn't murmurs or quiet whispers. There were no assumptions. It was actual videos. Film footage of her truth for the whole world to see. Jamison as he delivered endless blows to Ron's bloodied face, and then Colt as he shouted and said the actual word. *Rape*. There it was. Four letters shattered her entire world: *rape*, one word that changed her entire path. Everything. And now everyone knew.

Tears trickled down her face. Sobs escaped her lungs. Why? She shouldn't have come back here. There had to have been another way. Now she had been exposed. Everyone knew about her secret. Her painful secret. The paparazzi would be brutal. They loved a heartbreaker. It didn't matter who they hurt in the process, it was all about the story, and this one would sell a lot. Cheyenne Ford, country music's sweetheart had been raped. She was sick. The things they would uncover about her. It was too much to bear.

She slumped to the floor and tears continued to fall over her cheeks. The sound of her pain and all the years she had held it in were too loud. The hurtful memories crashed around her. The reality that she had tried to escape. Everything she had tried to avoid. Everything she had tried to hide. The noise of all those years was loud as they clamored against her head. Loud bangs of her truth escaped her mind. The shrill of her tears was so loud. Each sob was like her rib cracked into multiple hairline fractures. Split bones. Shattered tears against her skin. Her tomb of terrors that kept her up at night had been unsealed. Everyone knew. The secret had been delivered to the public without her consent. Her brain raced with images. The pain of this violation was loud. She'd been crying so hard, she didn't even hear the door open, hadn't heard anyone come in.

It wasn't until she felt Colt wrap her up into his strong arms that she realized she wasn't alone. She tried to pull away—the touch of another person was too much. She wanted to let the emotion drain from her body without the reality of someone else there to experience all of her sadness with her.

Colt pulled her in again. "Let me take care of you. Don't push me away this time, Cheyenne."

More tears fell. He shouldn't be here. It would only add

to the gossip mongers. It would make for an even bigger story, and his life would be upside down until they had exhausted him of his patience. Cheyenne knew how to deal with paparazzi; it was something she had learned. But Colt was not a part of that world. He wouldn't know or understand the first thing about these people and how relentless they were.

"You should go. It's best if you leave now."

"Cheyenne, I'm not going to leave you. And I'm not going to let you leave again." He ran his hand over the back of her head. "There are things we need to talk about."

"If they see you here … with me. They won't stop hounding you. It will be bad, I promise." He needed to understand that this wouldn't be just one night. They would keep following him, intruding on his life until they moved on to the next story.

Colt let out a laugh. "Darlin', nothing will be as bad as you leaving me again."

"Colt, I'm serious. You don't understand this world. They will dig up every piece of dirt on you and flash it out for the whole world to see. Do you want your mama to know all of your dirty secrets?"

"Now, what do you know about my dirty secrets?" He pulled on a strand of her hair.

Cheyenne rolled her eyes. "Colt, think about your mama and your family."

"The only person I'm worried about is you. Now, let me take you away, like I should have done back then." Colt pulled her to her feet.

"But what about Jamison?"

"I don't care about him right now. All I care about is you, and there is only room for two on my horse."

Just then, Jamison cleared his throat. He was fresh from the shower, his hair still wet, gray sweatpants slung low on his hips. "If she comes back in tears, you will be in the hospital this time."

The sides of Cheyenne's mouth pulled up. Colt gave a

slight nod. That was about as much of a truce as the two men would have. Colt led Cheyenne through the house and out the backdoor. They snuck across the lawn and into the small barn where two horses stood. This is why Jamison has rented the house; it came with two mares to ride. Little did they know, she would be using them to escape the press. Colt saddled the darker mare and helped Cheyenne up. He slid on behind her, and they exited the barn and out into the night sky.

A thick cloud covered the blanket of stars. There was only a crescent moon for light. The horse traveled at a quick pace through wide-open grass-covered fields into thick, dark forests. Colt said he would take her riding, and he was, but not the way either of them would have planned. If Colt hadn't had his arms wrapped securely around her waist, Cheyenne would have been afraid; she could not see far in front of them, and the terrain was rocky.

They rode for an hour until they reached a small cabin surrounded by tall pine trees. It was completely secluded. The stars seemed brighter here, countless specs of light on the black canvas. Colt slowed the horse and hopped onto the ground before he reached for Cheyenne. She fell into his body. She wanted so much to kiss him. But too many words had to be spoken before they could entertain the idea of the two of them together again.

"What is this place?"

"My get-away-from-it-all spot. When I wasn't trying to rope in women, I came here by myself to think."

The insides of Cheyenne's chest caved in. *Breathe. It's okay.* Time could not stand between her pain. It shouldn't hurt so much to think about him with other women, but it did.

He unlocked the door. It was pitch black.

"Stay here, I'll turn on the generator." A few moments later, the lights went on. The inside was small, quaint even, with caramel-colored wood floors and warm, planked walls. The floors were free of any rugs. A small wooden table sat alone in the kitchen, with two chairs and a couch in the living room, all were made of wood.

"Colt, did you make all of this?" She raised an eyebrow at him. She remembered he had been good with the saw in high school, but that was so long ago.

He took off his hat and hung it on a hook next to the door. "Yes, I had a bit of time on my hands back then."

"Wow, this is beautiful. I love it." She ran her fingers along the wall.

"Stay here, have a look around. I'll be back." Colt left her in the front room and her eyes explored all the wood-carved logs. Damn, he must have cut down a small forest to create this house and all of his furnishings.

"I want you to trust me, okay." Colt stood behind her and breathed into her ear.

"Okay," fell from Cheyenne's mouth. She didn't even have a chance to consider the alternate response, but it didn't matter. She wanted to trust Colt. She did.

He led her to the back of the house and into the bathroom, where a large metal tub sat filled with steam rising out from the water. Colt's lips pressed against the back of her head as he lifted the shirt from her chest. He unhooked her bra and left little kisses on her shoulders. His hands circled her waist and unfastened her skirt, letting it slide over her hips before he removed her panties.

Colt lifted Cheyenne off the wood floor and released her body into the water, then removed his clothes and slid into the water behind her. "I want you to tell me what happened." He breathed into her ear.

She took in a sharp breath. "What? I can't do that in a bath? I'm already exposed."

"No, darlin', you're safe with me. Tell me everything you've been holding in. Let me in." He picked up a sponge from the side of the tub and soaked it with the heated water before he ran it over her chest and paused in the center of her breasts. "Cheyenne, let me in."

Her insides shrunk. She was physically naked, and Colt

wanted her to bear it all to him. In this ultimate state of vulnerability. She had never been as exposed as she was here now in the tub and with Colt. The only rescue was her back being turned to him.

Cheyenne took in a deep breath. She closed her eyes and focused on the strong arms wrapped around her. She was safe. It was a long time ago. "Okay, I left because of what he did. I couldn't stay. He said he would keep doing it, and if I said anything, he would come up with a reason to arrest either you or me."

The pain she had held in for so long had been released from her tight grip. She had kept that secret down low in a place of forgotten painful history. Never had she wanted to bring it up. But there it was now. In the water.

He washed the sponge over her body. Soft smooth strokes over her neck and down her shoulders. Over her chest, he washed away the memory. The nasty, horrible event that had taken away so much from her and them. He ran the sponge down her stomach and over her thighs. He traced her calves and covered the bottom of her feet. He took away the pain with the gentlest of touch. A tear fell from her eye.

Colt leaned in closer to her and lifted her to nestle in his lap, then squeezed her body closer to his.

"I hate that you didn't come to me. I can't imagine what you went through. I just wish you would have given me a chance to fix it."

"Colt, I was seventeen and afraid." There was more to the story, buried even deeper in a place she couldn't go. Not now. Enough of her secret had been exposed for one night.

"I know, darlin', and that makes it even worse. You were so young, and I wish I could have protected you." He kissed her neck with soft, gentle kisses.

"I'm sorry I ran." She closed her eyes against the pressure that built behind them. She would not let herself think about how things could have been different, and what would have happened.

"It's not your fault. None of this is your fault. But I'm not letting you go again. I want you, Cheyenne." He turned her body around so that they faced each other.

"I don't know how we could work. There has been so much between us." She couldn't tell him the rest, too much time had passed ... but if she didn't, it would always be there, hanging between them, threatening their fragile attempts at happiness.

Colt glanced down. "Yeah, I'm sure between the two of us, we could fill up a stadium of ex-lovers, but that doesn't matter, darlin'."

Cheyenne focused on the bubbles that had begun to fade away ... just like the idea of them. Could they ever be something? She just didn't see how. Their worlds were too different. The crinkles of the suds were like a silent echo of a crowd before a show. She pushed the bubbles down.

"You would be on tour alone if that was the case."

Colt raised an eyebrow. "Darlin', I'm not going to ask for numbers, but let's at least be honest with each other. I know you haven't been celibate since you left my arms."

She took a deep breath. It was time to tell him. "I haven't had sex in eleven years."

Colt was quiet for a long time as he processed the information.

What was he thinking?

Say something. Anything.

"No one?"

Cheyenne. "Nope."

Colt glanced up at the ceiling. "Dammit. Now I feel like an ass."

Cheyenne reached for his arms. "I didn't want to be involved with anyone. I haven't let any other man close to me since that night, except for Jamison. I love him. He has been my everything. He held me up when I went to a dark place. After I left, I spiraled out of control, and J rescued me."

"Well, I owe him for that, but dammit, I hate that he got

to comfort you and got to be there for you." He pulled her hair to the side. "Cheyenne, don't leave me again." He leaned in and kissed her neck.

Shivers of happiness trailed over her shoulders and down her arms. She was almost clean ... almost all her secrets out.

Colt lifted her onto his lap, and she slid down onto his cock. Slowly, he eased into her. Her breasts rose out of the water, and he leaned his mouth in and captured her nipple. The apex of her thighs quivered, and she arched her back. Colt pulled her back in closer to her. "No, darlin', you're not going anywhere. You can't escape me anymore." His words sent fire through her chest and hit a deep spot that hadn't seen the light of day in eleven years.

Eleven years, and he already had her wrapped again. Like a ribbon around a present, she was ready to be signed, sealed, delivered, and ready to open on Christmas morning. Every day would be another visit to this special place.

She raised her body up and down as she glided her body over his erection. Over and over she played her body onto his like she was writing a hit song about her love for him. The passion that ran between them was like an orchestra of emotions that displayed in bright color lights in her mind. He was going to send her over.

She ran her hands through his dark hair and clawed at his back as he thrust deeper than she had tried. "Cheyenne." The cadence of his voice plucked against her ear. Little moments of what had been lost and forgotten rang up in a crashing sound of memories. Memories of what it was like to be with Colt and to be loved beyond a soft, soft shirt.

"Oh, Colt." She let out a cry. His body responded to hers, and his strokes increased. His rhythm was like a steel drum against her chest. His hands played over her skin like a fine-tuned piano. A melody of ecstasy danced in her heart and shot off a grand finale in her mind. He had broken her.

CHAPTER SIXTEEN

Bluebonnet Kisses

A bucket of wishes
A field full of blue
My love was always for you

Petals that dripped
Sparks of white
Everything back then
Seemed so right

Baby, we'll always have our bluebonnet kisses
Back when you called me your missus
You fulfilled every one of my wishes

Two kids so young and naïve
It hurt so much when I had to leave
I said goodbye and you held my hand
But I couldn't stay; it wasn't the plan

Baby, we'll always have our bluebonnet kisses
Back when you called me your missus

You fulfilled every one of my wishes

A field so pretty and blue
Cowboy, I always think of you
Even, years later as I fly by
I always knew you were my guy

Baby, we'll always have our bluebonnet kisses
Back when you called me your missus
You fulfilled every one of my wishes

"Thanks, Case, I owe you one." Colt could get back to the ranch to feed the horses and check on his cattle, but it would mean leaving Cheyenne here alone, and he would never do that. She wasn't ready to go back yet. Eventually, she would have to face it, but not yet.

"You owe me more than one. I've lost count. Will we see you at dinner today? Mama wants to see her too. You can't keep her to yourself forever."

Colt groaned. His brother was right. Colt could not keep them here forever, as much as he would like to. Things were simple here, just the two of them, no past, no future, just right now. But Colt would have to get back to the ranch soon. It was not fair to leave all the work to the guys. Colt should be there working beside them.

"I don't know. I will speak to Cheyenne. Thanks again, Case." Colt cut the call and slid the phone back into his pocket.

Cheyenne was still asleep inside. They had made love again, and then she had fallen asleep in his arms. He'd held her all night. It felt good, better than good, it felt right; the way it should be. He had never woken up beside her. All the times they had been together being stolen moments. Mostly in the daylight. This was different. This was the two of them as adults. No longer kids.

Colt went back into the bedroom. He wanted to hold her again. He loved this part as much as the sex; he loved the closeness too, the feeling that she belonged to him. He took off his jeans and slid into bed beside her. God, she was beautiful. Her hair fanned out over the pillow, flame against stark white.

Colt pressed his body against hers. He wanted to sleep like this forever, with nothing between them. He wanted to see her in the morning, and he wanted to come home to her every night. He took in a deep breath, smelling the clean apple scent of her hair. He was in deep. This wasn't a passing fancy. She was back in his life again, and he wanted her to stay. But did she?

She was holding back. He felt it. There was still an invisible barrier between them. He didn't press because … well, because he knew what happened last time he did: she ran. He knew when the sexual assault had happened. It wasn't hard to figure out. She changed overnight. The three weeks before she left, Cheyenne had been withdrawn and quiet. She never wanted to go out, and she didn't want to make love. He barely touched her, not even a kiss; she just shut down. He'd begged her to tell him what was wrong so he could fix it. And then she left. There was no goodbye. She was just gone.

"Good morning, Cowboy." Cheyenne smiled up at him, her bright blue eyes crinkled at the side.

"Mornin'. Did I wake you?"

She shook her head. "No, I've been up thinking. I need to go back into town."

"As soon as you do, my mama will want to have you 'round for dinner."

The smile disappeared as quickly as it appeared. "Does she hate me for the way I left you? I'm sorry, Colt. I wish I could have handled it differently, but …" Her voice trailed off. He waited for her to finish, but she didn't.

"Nah, my mama could never hate you. She always said you were the best thing that happened to me. She always thought I must have done something to screw it up."

Cheyenne's body went rigid. "No, no, it wasn't like that.

There was nothing you could have done."

Colt wanted to believe that. He had to ask. A hard lump formed in the back of his throat. "Do you forgive me? For not being there, for not protecting you?"

Cheyenne sat bolt upright. "Colt, this has nothing to do with you. I never blamed you. Ever. Not even for a second."

"The night it happened, I was gone. I should have been there. That was the night I went with Case to help deliver a calf, wasn't it?"

"Colt, don't do that. Don't play the 'what if' game. That never turns out well. Trust me, I have been playing it for eleven years."

Colt took her hand in his. "And do you ever ask what would have happened if I had told Case I couldn't help him? If I had driven you back from your grandma and not Ron?"

Cheyenne stared down at the patchwork quilt, tracing the pattern with her finger. "No. He had been following me. He told me. If it wasn't that night, it would have been another night. You helped Case because you're a good man. You have always been a good man. That's why I loved you."

Loved. Past tense. He tried to ignore the dejection that word brought. "What are you going to do next?" *Please say you're going to stay. Please say we will figure something out.*

"The statute of limitations has expired. I can tell you the exact moment it happened, ten years to the day after my eighteenth birthday. The moment I turned twenty-eight, he got a free pass." Her voice trailed off. "That was hard, that birthday was hard. Thank god I had J."

Hearing Jamison's name made his skin crawl. Finding out the man was gay did not lessen that. He still resented him. He was grateful that he had kept Cheyenne safe, but it should have been Colt. Those were years that belonged to him. They were stolen from him.

Cheyenne placed her hand on his chest. "I know you and J got off on the wrong foot, but I love him. He is my best friend. He got me through. That is why I wrote the song for him."

"I prefer the song you wrote for me."

"Which one?" Cheyenne's eyes were wide with curiosity.

"What do you mean, which one?"

"You still don't get it. Every love song I have ever written is about you. Listen to *Broken*. Every song on that album was written for you." She sighed, and let her eyes focus on the quilt.

Colt lifted her chin. He had to see her eyes. To really see her. To hear her response. Her words. "Really?"

"Really." She nodded.

"Well, now I can admit I own all of your albums." He laughed.

"You do?"

"Of course I do. I even went to one of your concerts in Louisiana."

Her eyes widened. "You were at one of my shows? I can't believe that. Ahh, now I am feeling self-conscience. Was I okay?"

"You're Cheyenne Ford—you were more than okay; you were amazing. The crowd loved you. They always do." Colt let the sides of his mouth pull up.

Her nose wrinkled. "The crowd doesn't know me. You have to know someone to love them."

Now was his moment. He could tell her he loved her, but we wouldn't. He couldn't. "Are you hungry? I brought peanut butter and bread. I can make toast."

Cheyenne looked out the window. "That would be nice. I'd love something to eat before going back into town."

"You know, on second thought, you don't need to go. You can stay here as long as you want. I can get supplies. Case is taking care of the ranch. My mom can wait to see you."

Cheyenne shook her head. "I need to face it. If I run, they will chase, and they will dig. They will dig up every little secret. I can't … I need to cut them off at the pass. If I give an interview, even one, it will take the wind out of their sales. It will be a nonstory. It is not interesting if I am willing to talk about it. I just need to do it—rip it off like a Band-Aid."

Colt hesitated. *Don't push.* But he had to. "What are you scared they will find out?"

Cheyenne blinked. It was clear she wasn't prepared for the question. She put on her stage smile, stood up, grabbed his hat, then put it on. She stood in front of him naked except for her smile and his hat. "The question, Cowboy, is what will they find out about you. Boy, I have been gone a long time. I am sure you have a lot of deep, dark secrets."

Colt smiled and shook his head. He wasn't going to be put off his question, no matter how cute she was.

Cheyenne bent over and picked up the twine that held together kindling. "Hands on the headboard," she commanded.

Colt laughed.

"I don't know why you're laughing. You're getting tied up, Cowboy." She wagged her finger at him.

"Am I now?"

"Where is your whip when I need it?" She peered around the room.

"Woman, you would hurt someone with a whip."

Cheyenne let out a soft giggle. "Only if you made me use it."

"Oh, is that the game we're playing?"

"No game, Cowboy. I'm going to get some secrets out of you." When Cheyenne shook her head, her hair moved enough to see the rosy peaks of her nipples. Fuck, she was sexy. She could tie him up and whip him and do whatever she wanted to him as long as she stayed with him.

Colt raised his hands above him and took hold of the wrought iron bars of the headboard. "Do your best, darlin'. I'm at your mercy."

The corners of Cheyenne's mouth pulled into a mischievous grin. "Do you trust me, Cowboy?"

"With my life," he replied without hesitation. She could do anything she wanted to him. Any limits didn't apply to her.

Cheyenne leaned over him to tie his hands together. Her nipple grazed his lips, and he captured the pink bud in his mouth and sucked.

"Oh no, you don't, Cowboy." Cheyenne pulled back. "I don't think so. You want this?" She rolled a nipple between her fingers. "You will have to answer some questions first." Her nipple went hard in her hand. Immediately his body responded, all the nonessential blood in his body redirected to his cock.

Cheyenne tightened the binding. "Feel free to fight against the rope. Only right that I mark you the way you marked me." She held up her wrists to show the faded red welts, then ran her hands over his chest, working his nipples into tight knots before tracing her hands over the deep ridges of his abs. "You are a fine specimen, I will give you that, Colt Clayburn. Honestly, how could you think I was with Jamison? I don't like blonds. Give me a tall, dark cowboy with black hair and big brown eyes. That is my thing. Where can I find one of those?" She laughed, and then leaned down and kissed him. She only let their mouths brush, but the moment he tried to deepen the kiss, she pulled back.

"First question. Hmm, let me see." She tapped her lips. "We will make it an easy one. Get your baseline reading like a lie detector. Consider me Maury Povich."

"I would rather not."

"Yes, a naked, red-haired, female Maury." She put her hands on her hips, which were curved to perfection.

"Now that is a show I would watch."

"I thought you would like that. I know you well. Now, stop distracting me. I am exposing all your secrets. First question: what is your favorite song?"

"'Bluebonnet Kisses,'" he replied in a heartbeat.

She shook her head. "No, not of my songs, of all songs. Think big, like of all songs ever written." She held out her hands as far as they would reach. "Think big."

"'Bluebonnet Kisses.'"

"Really? She squinted at him.

"Yes. Next question."

Her eyes narrowed. "You like that song because you always knew it was about you."

"Lucky guess. The entire song was about your first kiss. Seeing as I was the one you were kissing, it was a safe assumption."

"Actually, no, you weren't my first kiss."

Colt pulled against the rope. "Woman, you better be joking."

She shook her head. "I can tell you now. Because, well, you're tied up and all. You were not my first kiss. I was yours, but you were not mine."

"Who was it," Colt demanded. "I'll kill him." He was only half kidding.

"Ooh, fratricide, that is so Greek tragedy of you." Cheyenne laughed.

"You what? Cane? Are you saying you kissed my brother first?"

Cheyenne shook her head. "Not Cane."

"Cord. Did Cord kiss you? I will kill him. Son of a bitch."

"Not Cord."

"Case?"

She nodded. "Yep, after Sunday school. Mrs. Colley had just given a lesson on Samson and Delilah. The story is so sexy, don't you think? Anyway, you were home sick that day, and I grabbed Case and kissed him. I think I was the first and last woman to kiss him."

Colt studied her features. She knew too. "When did you figure it out?"

"Ages before you, Cowboy. Does your mama know yet?"

Colt shook his head.

"What about your brothers?"

"Nope."

Cheyenne frowned. "So only you and I know."

"Well, I like to hope he has sex, so presumably the men

he sleeps with would know."

Cheyenne bent over and kissed him again. "You got me off-topic again. Cowboy, you're so distracting, between the muscles and the tan and your stubble and your eyes." She sighed. "I want to tie you up once a week just to look at you."

"Only if I can do the same."

"Now, don't be lying. We both know if you tied me up, you wouldn't just be looking."

"True," he admitted.

"Right. Now that we have established a baseline, I can ask you some tough questions, and I'm going to sweeten the deal. I will reward every honest answer." A wicked grin spread across her face as she climbed into bed and settled between his legs. Slowly, she began to stroke his cock, up and down the shaft, and then she circled the head. "Why did you name your dog Jasper?" She lowered her head onto his cock, her tongue swirling around the crown while her fist pumped him. Oh god. She always knew how to do this. Nothing was like her mouth on him.

"I like the name."

Cheyenne moved her hand and sat up. "And the lie detector determined that was a lie." She shook her head. "Answer honestly and I will keep going."

"Yes, I named him after the egg baby we had in junior high."

Cheyenne rewarded him by returning her head to his cock. This time she took him deeper. Her hand cupped his balls, squeezing as she sucked. Oh god, that was good. She sucked and licked as her hands worked his balls. She gave the tip a quick peck before she sat up. "How long did you wait before you had sex with someone else?"

"Cheyenne, no." There was no way he was going to answer the question.

"Tell me, Cowboy, or that cock is going nowhere near these lips."

"No, Cheyenne."

"Okay, fair enough. We're done. Maybe if you spit in your hand, it will feel like my mouth. Or I know, warming lube, that will feel like me." She made a face. "But no, it wouldn't have the same suction. Hmm, what to do? What to do?"

"Twenty-three days." He anticipated the next question and answered, "I went to your parents' house. Your dad said he had just spoken to you on the phone and you weren't coming home. Ever. I drove to Houston. I met a woman in a bar. I don't remember her name. It was a one-night stand."

Cheyenne's mouth pulled down in a frown. Shit, he shouldn't have told her. Then, her head lowered again, and she sucked him harder, taking him deep in her throat. Oh fuck, that was good. He was going to come like that, down her throat.

She pulled back.

He groaned when she stopped. He was almost there. He could feel his balls begin to tingle. He needed to come.

"How many partners have you had?"

"I don't know. I haven't kept track."

"Ballpark."

Colt let out a frustrated laugh. "No, not that many, less than that. I couldn't fill an entire ballpark."

Cheyenne smiled. She stroked him with just enough pressure to keep him aroused. She had no intention of letting him come. This was payback for the barn, but he'd let her come.

He groaned again. His cock had never been this hard, this thick or long, and it was being wasted on pathetic half-hearted strokes of her hand. He needed to fuck her, either her mouth or her pussy. He just needed to be inside her.

"Did you ever think about me when you were with them?"

"Yes." More often than he would even admit to himself.

She lowered her head to his cock and sucked. Oh, sweet Jesus, that felt good.

"Oh, Cheyenne."

She sat up. "Have you ever thought about me when you touched yourself?"

"Of course. All the time. Most days in the shower."

The answer pleased her. She lowered her head again, but this time, instead of taking his cock into her mouth, she took one of his balls while her hand pumped him. The sensation sent a bolt of pleasure up his spine. "Oh fuck. Cheyenne, I need to come."

Cheyenne sat up again. "I'll let you come, but only if you admit that none of those women meant as much to you as I did." Her eyes were on his.

Colt couldn't take it anymore. He pulled free from the rope and grabbed Cheyenne's hips, then slammed her down hard on his erection. He filled her, not stopping until he hit the soft barrier of her cervix. Her eyes widened in surprise. "I can't wait. I need to be inside you. Ride me, Cheyenne. You know you're the only woman I have ever loved. I don't need to tell you that. You know."

Cheyenne smiled, then began to rock her hips against his, slowly lifting off of him before sliding back down his length in one fluid motion. Her pussy clenched around him each time, molding to him like a glove, a perfect fit. Her body was made for him.

"I won't last long," he warned. He couldn't make her come first this time. He didn't have the time or self-control. His body was spinning out of control, climbing toward ecstasy. He couldn't stop it, and he didn't want to. He just wanted her to ride him until he came in her soft body. He would make it up to her next time.

"Don't hold back, Cowboy. Come inside me."

With those words, he let go and came inside her with hot sprays, pumping high into her. Once finished, he pulled Cheyenne hard against his chest and held her. God, he loved her. Everything about her—the way she smiled, the way she laughed, the way she tasted. He needed to taste her again.

Colt rolled her over onto her back and spread her legs. Her pussy glistened, full of his cum. The sight was enough to make him hard again, but this was about her. He lowered his mouth onto her clit and began to suck as his fingers pumped inside her. She moaned his name, raising her hips off the bed, but he pushed her down so he could keep making love to her with his mouth.

"Oh, Colt," she screamed as an orgasm rocked her.

He kept licking. As one orgasm ended, another began.

"I can't," she protested, but she was already coming again.

Colt waited until the last tremor had faded before he sat up. *I love you.* The words were there in his mind and in his heart, but something stopped him from saying them out loud. Instead, he pulled her against him. They didn't need the words. In the same way, he didn't need to tell her she was the only woman for him. She knew. Even if he couldn't say the words, they both knew.

CHAPTER SEVENTEEN

There were paparazzi lined up outside the gate of Night Latch when Colt and Cheyenne arrived at the ranch. The large gates prevented anyone from entering, but it did not stop them from taking pictures through long-lens cameras.

Colt's chest tightened. It was his fault the world knew what had happened to Cheyenne. It was Colt on the video shouting it out. He would apologize again, but Cheyenne made him promise not to. Christ, she was strong. Anyone else would have crumbled by now, but she kept her head held high. She didn't complain about the photographers or all the media coverage. She didn't like it, but she never complained, she just took it in her stride like everything else. He admired that about her, along with so much else.

"Hey, Jasper." Cheyenne leaned down and rubbed the dog behind his ears.

"Welcome back," Case called from the doorway.

Cheyenne wrapped her arms around his brother. "Hey, Case, good to see you again."

"You too, Cheyenne. You look better than you did last night."

"I am. I feel good. Strong."

Colt closed the door behind them. "Thanks for taking

care of everything, Case."

"Don't worry about it. Your phone is ringing off the hook. I have no idea how they got this number. They're calling my office too." Case shrugged.

Cheyenne frowned. "I'm sorry, guys. You didn't sign up for this. It isn't fair."

"Cheyenne Ford, don't you dare apologize. This isn't your fault."

Colt put his arm around Cheyenne. "What he said. No more apologizing. This will blow over. We're good as long as you're holding up."

Cheyenne smiled. "I'm fine. What time do we need to be at your mama's?"

"In an hour. I'm going to head over now, unless you need me for anything." Case tapped his hands on the counter.

"No, we're good." Colt nodded.

"All right then, see you soon." Case lifted his hat and placed it on his head as he went through the front door.

Colt turned to Cheyenne and gathered her up in his arms. "We don't have to go to dinner."

"Yes, we do. I'm not going to hide away, and there is no way I am standing up your mama. I need to get back on her good side." She prodded his chest with her finger.

"Darlin', as long as you're on my good side, that's all that matters."

"I'm serious. I need your mama to like me. It's important."

She was talking like they had a future. He hoped they did, but he'd hoped they did then too. Things can change in an instant.

Cheyenne pulled back. "Right, I need to make something to take."

"My mama always has more than enough food. You must remember that."

"Colt, I am not turning up empty-handed. I am from Texas; I have manners." She turned on her heel and headed to the back of the house.

Colt followed her through to the kitchen. She searched through his fridge and cupboards, pulling out ingredients. "Chop the potatoes and I will make the sauce."

Colt smiled. This is what he imagined their future like, working side by side. It felt right, but then he remembered the photographers parked outside his gates. This wasn't the future they'd planned.

"Cowboy, did you forget how to use a knife?" Cheyenne smiled.

Colt kissed her forehead. "Such a perfectionist."

"Taste this." Cheyenne thrust a spoon into his mouth.

"Mmm, that's nice. Spicy." She could cook. When did that happen? The Cheyenne he knew could make cookies and Top Ramen.

Cheyenne moved on from the sauce and began putting together a potato salad, tossing together the ingredients, and then sprinkling crushed cashews on top.

"That looks great. Know what would make it perfect?"

Cheyenne rolled her eyes. "A steak on the side? I'm sure your mama will have made you a steak."

"Yep, with Angus from my ranch. You're back in Texas, darlin'. There is always going to be steak on the table."

"Come on, let's go." Cheyenne put a lid on the potatoes, then ran her fingers through her hair.

Colt couldn't help by smile. It made him happy how much she cared. They left through the front door and ignored the hollers from the road.

Cheyenne hopped in the passenger seat. Colt handed her the salad and slammed her door.

Flashes exploded around them when Colt pulled out of the driveway.

"You all right?"

Cheyenne nodded. "Just keep your eyes straight ahead, smile, and never answer a question. Don't even say no comment. Just pretend they're not there."

Colt smiled. He picked up her hand and kissed her

knuckles, then headed off toward his mom's.

When they arrived, there were more photographers camped outside his mom's house. Had they been there all night, or had they followed them? How did Cheyenne live like this all the time? It had to get old. He would want to move to a remote island.

The front door opened, and his mom stood in the frame. Her smile was enough to soften the annoyance of the photographers.

Colt's mom immediately threw her arms around Cheyenne. "Girl, it has been far too long." She planted a kiss on Cheyenne's cheek. Cheyenne visibly relaxed. His mama held no ill will toward her; Cheyenne must feel that. "How are your parents?"

"Good, real good. They are loving Florida. My mom runs a Paint Your Ceramic shop, and my dad golfs. They're really happy."

"That's great. Send them my love. And how is your brother?"

"Dustin is fine. They're still in Austin. Megan just had their second, a baby girl named Samantha Jean."

"After your mama. How nice is that? Do you hear that, boys? Dustin gave his mama a grandbaby, and they even named the baby after her."

"Subtle, Mama." Colt leaned down and kissed his mom's cheek.

"How are Cord and Cane? I have not seen them since I got back," Cheyenne asked.

"We won't see much of Cane until after the season is over. It is awful that they make him work on a Sunday. He never makes lunch anymore." She *tsked*.

"Mama, he is in the NFL—he is paid very well to *work* on a Sunday." Colt laughed.

Katrina brushed off Colt's comments with a shrug. "Even so. Sundays are for church and family. And don't get me started on Cord."

"Here, Cheyenne made a salad." Colt handed his mother

the salad before she could launch into a tirade about his baby brother. Katrina would never have chosen for her youngest child to be a bull rider, but he was, and he made a damn good living at it.

"Ooh, it looks delicious. It will go perfectly with the smoked tofu and corn on the cob."

"You made me tofu?" Cheyenne asked, clearly touched. She had always been happy to make do with bread and salad. "That was nice of you, Mrs. Clayburn."

"Now, you must call me Katrina. Or Mom." She winked.

Colt rolled his eyes. His mother was about as subtle as a freight train barreling down the tracks. Not that Cheyenne seemed to mind.

"I agree, Katrina, your boys need to visit you more often, and they need to give you grandbabies. And Katrina would make a beautiful name for a baby girl." Cheyenne caught his eye and gave him a naughty glance. She was ganging up on him with his mother and enjoying it far too much.

Colt wrapped his arm around Cheyenne's waist and whispered in her ear, "You're creating a rod for your own back. She will expect our firstborn daughter to be named Katrina."

Cheyenne went rigid. Her posture changed, her shoulders slumped, and the color drained from her face. The look of terror had returned. The one he saw when she saw Ron. What was wrong? Had the idea of having his baby upset her? Did she not want to have kids? Cheyenne patted her hair and eyed the ground. Or was it that she didn't want to have kids with him? The realization was a blow to the chest. It was okay for her to joke because it was just that, a joke, something that would never happen.

"I can't wait to try tofu," his mother announced.

"You're eating it too?" Case asked.

"We all are."

Colt shook his head. "With our steak. That seems like a weird side dish."

His mom laughed. "No, instead of steak. The whole

meal is vegan. Even dessert!" she announced triumphantly.

"Fantastic," Colt said, just managing to keep the sarcasm from his tone.

"I called Cheyenne's friend, and he gave me some recipes."

As if on cue, Jamison opened the screen door in the back and came in. Things just kept getting better. Jamison Keyes was in his mother's house.

"J." Cheyenne smiled as she crossed the room and threw her arms around him, kissing him on the cheek.

Colt was grateful to Jamison for protecting Cheyenne, but bizarrely, he was more jealous of Jamison now that he knew there wasn't a sexual component to his relationship with Cheyenne. Jamison had gotten to comfort Cheyenne when she needed it the most. Colt would always be jealous of that. But he knew if he said his feelings out loud, Cheyenne wouldn't be the only person bothered by his immaturity.

His mother sensed his unease. "Now, boys, I have seen the video of you fighting at Cheyenne's concert, but it is time to let bygones be bygones. Shake and makeup," Katrina commanded.

Colt looked from his mother to Jamison and back again. Jamison smiled a cocky smile and held out his hand. "I was just explaining to Katrina how there are no hard feelings on my part. And Case has seen it in his heart to forgive me for the black eye. Again, sorry, man. Time for us to man up and let this one go."

Case and his mother both smiled at Jamison.

Colt needed to be more mature and start acting on it, so he shook Jamison's hand.

"Let's eat. I made pureed celeriac," Katrina announced.

His mama had pushed the boat out. Vegetables in the Clayburn house usually came in the potato or carrot variety, with the occasional pea thrown in for color.

"Oh, that sounds wonderful, Katrina. Thank you so much for going through all this trouble. I love celeriac. J and

I had the best celeriac salad at this little café in Paris. When we got home, Jamison spent two weeks perfecting the recipe. He is an amazing cook. It is so good. J, you will have to give it to her."

"I'll do one better. I will make it for her. Come to our house next week, before we head back to Nashville. I will make you dinner to thank you for your hospitality. Case, you're coming too." Then he turned to Colt and added, "You too, Colt."

Our house? "Do you share a house in Nashville too?" Colt asked between clenched teeth.

Jamison's face broke into a broad smile. "Going on eight years. A house just doesn't feel like a home without Cheyenne in it. You know what I mean?"

Colt squeezed the glass of water in his hand a little too tight.

"Colt, your hand!" Cheyenne shrieked.

Colt glanced down at the broken glass. Blood gushed from his palm, pooling with the spilled water, and dripping on the floor.

Cheyenne acted quickly and pressed her napkin against his palm.

Case stood up. "Man, that's going to need stitches," he said when he examined Colt's hand.

Colt clenched his hand to quell the flow of blood, but it did nothing to stop the current.

"I'm fine," Colt protested when Case came back from his truck with his medical bag. The blood on his jeans and the hardwood floor told another story though.

"Boys, can you take the blood outside?" Katrina didn't even look up from her plate of potato salad. Raising four boys had hardened her to the sight of blood. They were always coming in with cuts and bruises. She would not even bat a lid at a broken bone. Organs had to be hanging out for his mother to show any concern.

Colt pushed back from the table and followed his brother to the back porch. "It's fine. Just put a Band-Aid on it."

"Man, this needs at least a couple of stitches."

"You're not a doctor. You don't know that."

"No, I'm a vet, which is exactly what you need because you're a horse's ass."

Colt scowled. "He shouldn't be here. Mama should never have invited him."

Cases wiped away the blood on Colt's hand. "What exactly has he done to you?"

"He busted my lip for starters."

"Um-hum, and you gave him a black eye and bloodied his nose. What else you got?"

"He gave you a black eye too." His voice was thick with indignation. Case should be just as pissed as he was, but somehow he wasn't.

"I don't have any local anesthetic in my bag. I will have to take you into my office."

"No, just do it."

"Colt, don't be an idiot."

"Just sew it up and be quick about it."

"You are an ass, you know."

Colt watched as Case laced the thick black thread through the cut, drawing the edges together, tying off each knot.

Once done, Case inspected his handy work. "Your days as a hand model are over, but you'll live." He placed a bandage over the wound and taped it in place. "Legally, I am not supposed to do this, so it never happened. If it starts to itch or look infected, let me know and I will give you some antibiotics. Keep it dry, and don't chew at the stitches."

When Colt didn't laugh, Case said, "Sorry, vet humor."

Colt shook his head. "Work on that, or you'll always be single." Colt left his brother and walked back to the house and toward Cheyenne.

"Can I speak to you for a second, Cheyenne," Colt asked, trying to keep his tone neutral but not quite managing it.

Cheyenne looked up and smiled. "Yeah, sure, can you give me two seconds? I am going to help your mama serve up the apple crumble. She even got vegan vanilla ice cream to go with it." Her eyes were bright with excitement.

Colt did not answer; instead, he took her hand and pulled her through to the bathroom at the end of the hall.

"What's wrong? How is your hand?"

Colt was silent. He locked the door behind them, and then pulled her hard against him. "I need you, Cheyenne."

Her eyes widened in surprise. He took her face in his hands and kissed her as he pushed her up against the wall. His hands and mouth were all over her, licking her neck and pulling up at her skirt.

"We can't do this, Colt, someone will hear us." Cheyenne laughed, her cheeks flushed.

"I can be quiet—can you, darlin'?" Colt ran his finger over her lips.

Cheyenne bit at the tip of his finger and licked it. "A challenge to who can be quieter? You're on, Cowboy."

Colt turned her around so she was facing the basin in front of the mirror. Cheyenne held on to the vanity as Colt tugged down on her panties. "I need to be inside you." It was an explanation and an apology. This wouldn't be pretty or romantic. This was about need. He had to be inside her, feel that connection again. Nothing else mattered when he was inside of her. The rest of the world, their past, everything, it all just disappeared. They were just two people that needed each other.

Cheyenne's gaze caught his in the mirror. Desire hooded her eyes. She wanted this too. He ran his hand over the curve of her ass. "Next time it will be slow and sweet," he promised. "But this time I want you too much to go slow."

Cheyenne nodded her approval. With a powerful thrust, he filled her, and her eyes widened. Colt leaned over and kissed her neck, forcing himself to slow down and enjoy the sensation of her pussy stretched tight around his cock. He closed his eyes and breathed her in. She felt so good, so perfect, so tight and wet and hot. He told himself to go slow, and for three strokes he did, but when he caught her eyes in the mirror, the depth of something more than heated passion broke him. There was no holding back then; he couldn't. He tried, but there was no fighting it, the need to fill her, mark her, claim her. Over and over he pumped into her, his eyes never leaving hers. He watched in the mirror as he fucked her. The way the color rose in her cheeks, climbing up her neck, the way her nipples strained against the thin material of her tank top.

He needed more of her, always more. He could never get enough of her. A lifetime would only begin to take the edge off. He didn't want it to end, but he knew he was close. With a final thrust, he came inside her. Her body quivered against his skin, and Colt pulled her in tightly against his body. *I love you.*

Cheyenne sighed. "Let's go make our apologies so you can take me home."

"What about your vegan ice cream?"

"I have had vegan ice cream before. I have only woken up to you once."

Colt spun her around and kissed her. God, he loved her.

He let Cheyenne leave the bathroom before he followed a minute later so it would hopefully look less like they had been screwing over the sink.

When he made his way back, Cheyenne was in the kitchen hugging his mom. Jamison caught his eye. "Just so you know, I am not going anywhere. I have been with Cheyenne a long time. What I have with Cheyenne goes deeper than anything you will ever have. You get her body. I get everything else. When you make her cry, I'm the one wiping away her tears. I'll still be by her side when it is some other horny cowboy she is fucking in the bathroom."

Cold shook his head. *Walk away.* But a voice that he couldn't ignore told him he was right. "Go away. Find another woman to be your beard. Cheyenne is mine now.

She doesn't need you."

Jamison tackled him and pushed him against the wall. Framed photos fell from their hooks, shattering the glass.

"Boys!" Katrina shouted from the kitchen. Cheyenne ran into the hall. She stood between them, her hands held out to keep them apart. Both men itched to get another blow in, but neither would move with Cheyenne separating them.

"Enough!" she shouted. "I am sick of all this chest-pounding bullshit. Man up, both of you. Just stop it." Anger flashed in her blue eyes.

Neither of them spoke as Cheyenne looked from Jamison to Colt. "J, go back to the house." Cheyenne spun on her heel to face Colt. "Don't look so satisfied with yourself, Cowboy. I'm not going home with you either."

"What?" Jamison and Colt said in unison.

"Katrina, can I stay with you tonight?"

"Of course."

"Mama," Colt protested. "There is an army of photographers camped out wherever she goes. I am not going to leave her alone."

"Your brother will stay with us tonight. Won't you, Case?"

Case shot his mother a don't-drag-me-into-this look before he ran a hand through his hair and sighed. "Fine. Maybe it is for the best if y'all get some space."

Space? From Cheyenne? They had been apart for the last decade. The last thing they needed was space. Jamison's focus was on the ground. They were both being like teenagers. The remorse seemed mutual. The sound from Jamison's phone cut the tension. He stepped outside to answer it.

"Cheyenne, please," Colt began. "Don't do this. Come home with me to the ranch. We need to talk."

Cheyenne held up her hands in exasperation. She stared at him for a long time as if she was considering her options. "Promise me you won't lay a hand on Jamison again."

"Darlin', you have no idea—"

"Promise me, or I will be spending every night I have left in Texas with Case and your mama."

She had him over a barrel. Of course he would agree to it. He would agree to anything to keep Cheyenne in his life, in his bed. "Fine," he muttered between clenched teeth.

"Say the words out loud."

Colt had said the same words to her once, but then it was more fun. For starters, they were in a barn about to have sex.

"I promise to not hit Jamison no matter how much of an asshole he is or what he says to intentionally piss me off."

Cheyenne rolled her eyes. "Honestly, Colt. You had more self-control as a teenager."

Colt ran his hands through his hair. He might have had some more self-control back then, but he also had the guarantee that Cheyenne belonged to him. There was no worry that she was about to leave his life forever. Little did he know.

Jamison returned moments later; his brows were furrowed. "Your phone is off, princess."

"Yeah, reporters were calling. I don't even know how they got my number. I switched it off."

"That was Dennis and Maggie. Jenn has spiked a fever. They want to know if you will come to Houston to see her. She wants to see you."

The color drained from Cheyenne's face. "Let me get my bag."

"Is this the little girl with cancer? I'll take you," Colt said.

Cheyenne spun to face him, the same look of sheer terror marred every feature. "No! No, Jamison can take me. I … need to go. Jamison will drop me off at the ranch tonight. I can't … you can't … I just need to go."

Colt watched as Jamison wrapped his arm around Cheyenne's shoulders and walked her outside, away from him.

CHAPTER EIGHTEEN

No hospital ever has an appearance of happiness. Even though it is a place that is supposed to make people better, it never portrays the essence of health. It is always bleak and gray, even with the bright-colored letters out front. It was still a downer to enter in through the double glass doors, especially today; Jenn had spiked a fever, and now even if they had a match, it wouldn't matter. She wouldn't even be able to accept it while being sick.

Cheyenne clenched her fists. Jamison had lost a trail of paparazzi en route to the hospital, but somehow a slew of them were at the front of the doors, their cameras out, already flashing. How did they do that? Always knew where she was. Cheyenne passed them without a glance, as if she couldn't even see them through her dark shades. She did not need sunglasses—it was a night—but she couldn't let anyone see her eyes in case she cried. She was trying not to, but the pressure was already building.

Jamison guided her through the doors, past the group of whispering nurses, and straight to the elevator. Inside the hospital, they were safe from the cameras, but it didn't matter, Jenn wasn't safe. She was in the danger zone. This is why they had called Cheyenne. They wanted to make sure

Jenn got to see her in case. No. That couldn't happen. No matter what.

The elevator jolted to a stop, and Jamison held the door as Cheyenne made her way through and down the hall to Jenn's room.

The nurse stopped them outside. "Here, you have to put these on. We can't have any more germs in the room."

Cheyenne and Jamison put on the hair cover, face mask, and gloves. She would put on a Hazmat suit if it meant Jenn would be safe.

Cheyenne's insides were like open wounds that had been slashed with a dull razor blade and acid poured over them. The pain was intense, but she was numb. She shut out the desire to scream and cry, to kick and plead with all things merciful, give Jenn a chance, spare her. Someone.

Dennis and Maggie were each planked on either side of Jenn's bed, each holding one of Jenn's hands. Everyone had the same form of protection.

Cheyenne forced a tear back. Do not be sad. Not in front of this brave little girl. She deserved more than that. Cheyenne composed herself, then rushed over to the side of the bed.

"Hey, sweetie, thanks for inviting me to your costume party." Cheyenne forced a voice of happiness to push past the hospital mask.

Jenn glanced up at her and smiled. "You came." Dark circles encased her golden-brown eyes.

"Of course I came. I wouldn't want to miss out on the fun. I've got some pens in my purse. Maybe you can drop a happy face on my mask for me?"

Cheyenne began to dig in her purse, when a nurse rushed to her side. "No, she can't touch anything from your purse."

Cheyenne's shoulders slumped. "That's right. I'm sorry."

Jamison picked up a pen from the side table. "Can she use this?"

"Yes, that's been sterilized." The nurse nodded.

Jamison handed the pen to Jenn. "Here you go—make sure you make a really silly face. Cheyenne is always being goofy."

Everyone laughed. It was like the room had forgotten why they were all there covered in light blue masks and gloves.

Cheyenne squatted down next to the bed and leaned her face up so Jenn could reach her mask. Jenn drew a big mouth and a word bubble to the side of it.

"Uh-oh, Cheyenne, looks like Jenn is going to write out a speech for you on your face." Jamison laughed.

Cheyenne waited patiently as Jenn worked the pen over her mask. She didn't want to move and mess up whatever it was that Jenn was drawing.

"There, it's done." Jenn placed the pen down on her bed.

The room was silent. Cheyenne glanced around. Not a word was spoken.

"Well, go on then. Tell me what it says?"

All eyes withdrew from Cheyenne's face, but she caught Jamison. He wouldn't dare to ignore her plea.

"It says, *This Isn't Goodbye*." He pressed his lips together.

Cheyenne's heart stopped. Did she know? No one would have told her. No one. Cheyenne stood up. It wasn't possible. Jenn just didn't want this to be a farewell. That's all. She just wanted to keep the party going.

"No, baby girl, you're right; this isn't goodbye." She patted down Jenn's hair. "I'm going to go and get my journal, the one we talked about. I'm going to get it, and we're going to sing a special song. Together, you and me."

As Cheyenne began to make her way toward the door, another nurse came into the room. "Visiting time is over."

No, they just got there. Couldn't they make an exception, extend the hours? She wasn't ready to say goodbye. Cheyenne eyed the floor. *No tears. Don't do it. Be brave. Be brave for Jenn.* "You're going to get better. You will. I promise."

Inside, Cheyenne punched her stomach. Never make

promises you can't keep. And she'd done just that. She made a promise to a sweet, beautiful girl that there was no way Cheyenne could keep. Even if she was able to find a bone marrow match, it didn't mean Jenn would get better. Dammit. Why did she do that? Why had she said that? She wished she could take back those nine words of hope. It wasn't fair to lie to someone in their hospital bed. It wasn't right. Cheyenne knew better.

Jamison wrapped his arm underneath Cheyenne's shoulders, and with as much grace as possible, led her out of the room. Cheyenne made a silent promise to herself to come back before it was too late. Time was of the essence. Every molecule in that hospital room echoed the inevitable.

"Do you want to go back to the house with me," Jamison asked. "I'll let you wear my shirt, and I will snuggle you until you fall asleep."

Cheyenne tried to smile, but her face wouldn't cooperate. Normally that would be exactly what she needed, but not tonight. She needed to be with Colt. He was the one she needed to hold her. She glanced at the clock. He would be asleep by the time they got back to Cut and Shoot because he was always up before dawn to start his workday, but it didn't matter. Even in his sleep, Colt held her, his body always found hers and molded to her. It was like they were cut from the same cloth.

When they arrived at Night Latch, photographers lined the gates, shooting pictures as Jamison drove through. It wouldn't end until another story took them away, or until Cheyenne gave them what they wanted, her story. It was hers to tell and theirs to sell. Capitalism in the form of emotional warfare.

Jamison slowed the car. "Are you sure you want to stay here tonight?"

Cheyenne nodded. "Yeah. I love you, J. Thank you for always having my back."

Jamison leaned over and kissed her forehead. "I always will, princess. You will always be the most important woman in my life."

Cheyenne smiled. "I hope not. I hope you find Mr. Right and get married and have a daughter with your eyes. She would be beautiful. And god helps any man who messes with her. You will be a great daddy, J."

Sadness tugged at her heart. Somewhere in her mind, she always acknowledged she was holding Jamison back. He was an openly gay man, or he had been until being her cover dragged him back into the closet. Letting people assume J was her lover made her life easier. No one asked questions or pushed, so Jamison had been discrete, never having serious long-term relationships that would jeopardize the façade they had created. He had done that for her; he had put his life, his happiness on hold. It wasn't fair. She should never have let it happen. She never asked, but Jamison would always do whatever it took to protect her, even at the expense of his happiness. Not anymore. She needed to stop being selfish. "Jamison, I want you to go on a date. With a man," she added hastily.

"Of course it would be a man." He laughed. "That's kind of the way it works for me."

"I'm serious. You need to start dating if you are going to find Mr. Right and have your beautiful green-eyed daughter."

Jamison let out a long stream of air. "What about when we leave? When we're back in Nashville and it is just you and me? What then?"

She knew what he was asking. Would she still feel the same way when it was over with Colt? The question tore at her insides. But it was a fair question. She wasn't sure if she knew the answer. So much had happened between them, made her wonder if it was possible to ever really make a go of things. She loved Colt with everything she had, but it seemed like their fate had been sealed a long time ago. Jenn's hospital visit had left her with a more remorseful reality of life than she wanted to process. Colt and Cheyenne might have been good together once. But now, were they just pretending that they could make it work? Besides, fairytales aren't forever. Reality would seep through the hazy dreamlike way she was around Colt. With no concerts to perform or contracts to contend with. Cheyenne had a life outside of Cut and Shoot. Jamison needed to have one too.

"I want you to have what I have had with Colt. The great sex and the connection." *And the love.* She couldn't say the word, but she loved him. He was the only man she had loved like that.

"I have great sex."

Cheyenne smiled. "I want you to find love. And I have no doubt sex with you would be amazing. How could it not be, I mean, it's you?"

"True."

"Good, it is settled. Find a man." Cheyenne pecked him on the cheek, and then slid out of her seat and slammed the door. She waved to Jamison, then headed toward the other man in her life, the one she currently needed: Colt.

CHAPTER NINETEEN

Colt listened to the car pull up on his gravel drive, and eventually leave. Cheyenne was here. He should feel relieved that she was home, that she came back to him, but he wanted the intimacy of being the person she chose to comfort her, and she still wasn't letting him in.

Cheyenne opened the door to the bedroom. His back was to her. She was naked when she slid into bed.

"Colt," she whispered, but he did not respond. There was no point. He finally realized that. He didn't let himself move, no matter how much he wanted to wrap his arms around her and make love to her, and then hold her all night. There was no point. He was in deep. He had let himself free fall into her, but she held back. It wasn't just what happened with Ron. There was something else.

Colt couldn't give anymore. She had all of him. He waited for her breathing to slow, and then he waited even longer just to make sure she was asleep, only then did he turn to her. He wrapped his arms around her and breathed her in. He could hold her in their sleep. It would be just this. Nothing more. That's the way how this story went. It was clear to him. It was probably clear to her too. The time for them was back in high school. It didn't matter about the years and things they could have had. It was not going to happen, and this charade needed to come to an end.

It seemed like only a few minutes had passed when his alarm went off. Sleep was for the dead. Just like his hopes. Colt climbed out of bed and made about the room with a quickness. He didn't want to wake her and, even more, didn't want to talk.

CHAPTER TWENTY

The horse was soft and gentle. Colt said Buckles was the best stallion for her to have on film. Even though he and Jamison urged her not to do the interview, she knew this was the way it had to go. If she faced this situation head-on, then she could be the voice, not the media. If they got her soundbites and her words, she could be her truth instead of all the suggestions and accusations. Dammit, she couldn't take any more accusations that she wanted it. How sick. Who writes that crap? No, it needed to stop. It was time to stand up and do what was right. She owed it to the countless victims who didn't have a voice or the access to media that she did. It was time for her to be brave for them. And it was time to be brave for herself and the seventeen-year-old Cheyenne who had been so lost and unsure of what to do or who to reach out to.

Jamison pulled Cheyenne into his body and ran his hand over the back of her hair. "You don't have to be strong for anyone else." He kissed her forehead.

Colt took off his hat and raked his fingers through his hair. The vein in his neck flexed. He slammed the hat back on his head and bit his lip. Cheyenne eyed him. Steam swirled around him. He reminded her of the day of the

Texas Get Registered Concert.

"Hey, are you okay?" Her eyebrow raised in question. He had put up a fight about the interview too but finally caved when Cheyenne asked if she could do it on his ranch.

She agreed to do one interview with Lucy Tanner from KPRC local news, and they would air it on all the national networks. Cheyenne had watched a few of Lucy's segments, and she seemed nice enough. Not a hard hitter. All Cheyenne wanted to do was answer the questions and move on. Get past this moment and let it go away. Somebody else needed to take the spotlight. A new baby or an engagement, let that be the focus of the country music scene.

"They're here," Max, one of Colt's right-hand men, called into the barn.

Colt reached for Cheyenne's hands and led her to the back of one of the stalls. The place where he had laid her down on a bed of hay a few days earlier.

"Cheyenne, I admire your strength, I do, but it's okay to cancel."

She rolled her eyes. "Come on now, I'm not going to cancel. I agreed to do it. It's not a big deal. Quick and easy. I've done hundreds of interviews before." She threw on her stage smile. "I'm a natural."

Colt smiled back, but it didn't reach his eyes. He had a practiced smile too. It was there on his face. Was he worried about this interview or something else? Cheyenne swallowed.

A shiny blond-headed man in a custom tourist country attire strolled into the barn and tipped his hat to Cheyenne. "Hey there, darlin', are you ready for our chat?"

Cheyenne jerked her head back. *Darlin'* was reserved for Colt only. And who was this man? Where was Lucy? Cheyenne hadn't agreed to anyone else.

"I'm sorry, who are you?" She strode toward him, gaining her composure with each step.

Colt and Jamison planked her side. If she had any fear, it would have been washed away with these two giants next to her.

"I'm Taylor Thomas. I'm the head anchor for KPRC. Lucy, unfortunately, couldn't make it. I do apologize for that."

"Huh, is that right?" Cheyenne rubbed her lips together. A vibration sounded from her pocket. "Excuse me, will you, please?" She took a step away from the three men and glanced at the caller ID. It was Owen Hayes, the PI she had hired.

"This is Cheyenne Ford."

"Hi, Ms. Ford."

"Cheyenne, please."

"Yes, Cheyenne, I'm sorry. It's Owen. We got the results back, and Ron is not the father or a donor match."

Cheyenne grabbed onto the bale of hay and squeezed tight to the straws. They fell through her hands. Each grip she attempted came up empty. Her throat closed tight. She tried to utter a thank you. Something. But it was too dry. Everything was dry: her face, the hay, her throat. *Breathe.* Her eyes were the only thing wet on her body. *Blink. Focus. Think. Speak. Do something.*

Thankfully, Jamison moved forward and reached for her phone. "Hello, this is Jamison ... Yes, I see ... Okay. Thank you." He slid the phone into his pocket and squeezed Cheyenne tight as he kissed her head. "It's a good thing, Cheyenne."

Cheyenne's hands trembled. Her fingers tingled. She swallowed hard. The news hit her like a gust of wind on a calm day. Everything had moved around in her mind. She needed to settle herself. She clenched her fists and jutted out her jaw, then rolled her neck. When she turned to go back out again, she saw Colt approaching from the front of the barn; his brows were furrowed.

"What's going on, Cheyenne?" Colt stared down at her.

Guilt washed over her. She didn't want it to be Ron, but if he had been a match, that would have been worth it for Jenn.

"Cheyenne? Do you want me to cancel? Say the word and I'll clear everyone out."

"Yes, cancel. She didn't agree to an interview with this guy, and I don't like him." Jamison's eyes glared in the direction of Taylor.

Colt grunted. "Well, that's something we have in common." He turned on his heel. "Hey, partner, I'm sorry, but Cheyenne hadn't planned on meeting with you." He tipped his hat at the guy.

Cheyenne stood up and found her voice. "No, it's fine. I'll do the interview." She reached for a brush from the shelf and stalked to Buckles. She was going to brush out her answers. That had been the plan. She could do this. This was just another performance. Cheyenne put on her stage smile and nodded. "Let's get started, okay?"

"Yes, ma'am. Let's do this." Taylor rushed over to her side and waved in his camera crew.

The lights were placed all over the barn, and Cheyenne ignored the flashes and sound tests. She stood still as the microphone was attached to her light blue button-down top blouse that she'd paired with jeans and her favorite Stetson boots.

"So, Ms. Ford," Taylor began, his eyes sparkling with a false sense of comfort. There was nothing nice about this man. He was one of those hard hitters that Cheyenne had wanted to avoid. Oh well. She was in boot deep at this point. No way to turn back. Not on film. No way.

"Cheyenne, please." She swiped some hair off her face.

"Cheyenne, it's recently been presented to the media that you were assaulted several years ago."

Cheyenne's eyes widened. Okay, so he was going to start with a bang. "That's right."

"Why didn't you come forward when it supposedly happened?" Taylor tapped a pen against his lip.

Cheyenne blinked for a second. "I was seventeen at the time and afraid. I didn't know what to do."

"It never occurred to you to report it to the police?"

Again, his pen rested against his lips.

"Ron was the police, so no, that didn't occur to me." The idea of the brush and smooth strokes was long gone. This was an attack. She couldn't concentrate on the horse's mane. This was about survival. She had to make sure she stayed focused on these questions and her answer. This man was out for blood. He wanted to catch her to have a soundbite that would be worse than all the murmurs.

"Did you tell anyone?"

Cheyenne glanced at the hay that lay against the floor of the barn. "No, I didn't, I was scared and embarrassed."

"What do you say to those who think you might have been embarrassed because maybe you kind of liked it?"

Cheyenne dropped her jaw, and Colt made a move to lunge for Taylor, but Jamison held him back and whispered something in his ear.

"No, I most certainly didn't like it. I was handcuffed to a pole, beaten, and assaulted. Does that sound like something you might enjoy?" Cheyenne stood up. "This interview is over." She ripped the microphone off her blouse and stormed out of the barn and to the Escalade, kicking up the dust in her way.

She needed to get far away from all of this. It was too much. From the rearview mirror, she noticed Jamison and Colt each had an arm of Taylor's and were dragging him toward the rented truck he had driven in.

She didn't care. Taylor was an asshole. The world was full of them. Cheyenne didn't have time for assholes today.

Suddenly, she couldn't breathe. Regret, remorse, and guilt pumped through her veins. Yes, she was seventeen, but maybe she should have said something back then. Maybe if she had told someone things would be different now. God, eleven years' worth of difference. So many things would have been changed. If she had just been brave ... if she had stood up and said something to someone, just one person. That's all it would have taken. But she had been afraid. If she had told her mama or dad, then her dad would have killed Ron, and then he'd have ended up in prison. No, she couldn't have that. It was best that she had left. Even if meant that she had given up Colt. She couldn't put anyone else at risk. It was her fall, her tragedy to contend with. No one else.

Though now was not the time to contend with what-ifs. There was something she needed to do. She took the backroads to her parents' old house. It was the same from the outside: big white porch swing, green shutters—everything that used to make her happy. Home. But it hadn't been sweet and comfortable after that night. She had had to get as far away as possible from it. Her parents had long since moved, but she'd bought the house from them in secret. Even they didn't know about it. They didn't know she was the new owner. The one that paid way over the asking price. Only Jamison knew. Some days she dreamed of a match being lit and the whole thing set ablaze, but she had never been back to make that happen, until today.

She slammed the car door and ran up to the front porch. It still squeaked in all the same spots. Cheyenne knelt and peeled up the loose piece of wood to the right of the door for the spare key. Still there. She stuck the key in the slot and took the place. Not much had changed. Her parents had left most of the furniture. She had the contract written to give extra money as an incentive for each piece of furniture that was allowed to stay with the house. The idea of all of it being left made it somewhat easier on her. She didn't want them to have any of this with them in Florida. It would be better if it could burn here.

She climbed the steps and tugged on the attic string. The only reason this house wasn't demolished was for what lay in the attic: her high school journal. All her happy memories had been written down along with a few of her first songs. But she had also written down what had happened that night. Cheyenne couldn't bring herself to destroy the journal, because that meant she would have to let go of all those nice moments that had been saved. It wasn't fair to get rid of those. Now, she was stronger, no longer a naïve, frightened girl. No, she was a woman, and she would do this. She was ready to rip that page out, the bad one. The horrible one. The one that shattered her world. The black ink had long been dried, and it was time to remove it permanently.

Cheyenne sat on the floor of the attic and dug through the box from her bedroom. She had placed this carton full of memories here the day she left. The framed photos of her and Colt. She smiled at the four years' worth of homecoming mums that he had given her when the bells jingled as she sifted through items.

To my Texas Darlin' … I'll love you forever.

A tear caught on her lashes. *Forever.* Colt had always told her he would love her forever, and then she left. Her heart was full of bittersweet memories and wishes of what could have been. All of her high school moments and pieces of her heart were in this container. She needed to get the journal and get out.

She sifted through her stack of books and found it. In the worn purple leather-bound journal on the front, she had written *Cheyenne's Deep Thoughts.* A journal was full of memories and a dash full of tears. These pages were filled with her high school years. Colt had seen it one time and teased her about it ever since. Tried to tickle her to submit to him and let him read it. But she wouldn't ever. No, these were her secrets. Her quiet memories. They were filled with all of her firsts. The night they had snuck out together. Their first kiss. The first time he had laid her down in the bluebonnets. The day they exchanged *I love you*s. It was all there. It has sat in this dusty attic for years. It waited to be dug up.

"Cheyenne."

Cheyenne screamed.

Colt rushed to her side. "Hey, darlin', I didn't mean to startle you."

Cheyenne let out a laugh. "Cowboy, I almost had a heart

attack."

"Well, that makes two of us. Jamison had your phone when you took off, and the idea of you out there alone really did me in."

"I had to get away."

He sat down on the floor and pulled her into his lap, trailing soft kisses against her head. "Are you okay?"

"I am now." She turned her neck so their heads could meet. She should tell him now. It was the right thing to do. It was the moment that needed to exist. Cheyenne pulled back and stared at him. His shoulders were squared, muscular, and so large. She wanted to lay her head against his chest and pretend, not confront the reality of what needed to be said.

God, she loved him. It never went away. And now, back in his arms, she didn't want to lose his love. She knew he loved her too, but he wouldn't afterward, so she needed to have him one last time before it was over. It was wrong, but she didn't want to do the right thing, not anymore, not with Colt. She wanted him too much and needed this memory. This last one where he still looked at her like she could do no wrong. It was dishonest, but it was the only way she could be true to herself. Cheyenne was going to be selfish.

She turned her body and wrapped her legs around his waist. "Make love to me, Colt, please." She forced herself not to cry. She didn't want to seem weak. She needed him to want this moment too. This last time.

"Darlin', you don't have to ask. I'll always make love to you."

His lips met hers with a soft force. She opened her mouth to him, and he captured her tongue. She released her own to dance with his. This was it. God, she would miss his kisses that swept her away.

She ran her hands through his hair, and he unbuttoned her blouse. She pulled off his shirt over his dark hair. Every part of him was a pure man. He was a man. He was her man at this moment. His muscles flexed along his chest and arms as he undressed her. His hands reached over her hips and slid off her pants, then tore his own. She knelt over his body and trailed her lips over his chest. He was so strong, so built. She needed him. She would always need him and his strength. She should have trusted in him before. A lump formed in the back of her throat, and she pushed it down. *Focus.* Her mouth made a path to his heart, and she paused. His arms held her over him.

"Cheyenne, what's wrong?"

"Nothing, Colt, I just need you."

"You've got me. Darlin', you've got me forever." He tipped up her chin so their eyes met. She leaned down so they could kiss again, and she slid off her panties and reached for his cock. He was going slow, but his erection was hard and thick. Cheyenne needed him inside of her. She wanted to connect with him, to be intertwined with each other. To be more than two separate people. She wanted to be one with him before her emotions gave way. *Focus.* She needed to be strong at this moment, so she could look back on it and remember this last time with Colt.

There was no question he was ready. She took it upon herself to ease onto him. At some point, she tried to rush, but Colt rolled her over and retracted, then entered her again with slow thrusts as his warm eyes full of concern bore into hers. He was reading her. It was like she had left her journal open for him to page through, and he was. His eyes ran over her face as he worked his body deeper into hers.

"Cheyenne, talk to me. Tell me what it is." He pulled her into his lap, still deep inside her. urging her to speak with each push.

"Please, let's just finish."

"Just finish? Cheyenne, what is it?"

His eyes stared into hers. She couldn't take the look in his eyes, so she looked away toward the back of the attic, where a small wooden piece caught her eye. No. It couldn't be. Her insides collapsed. She fell against his chest and tears trickled down her face as her body shook. Dammit. She messed up. She was wrong. She should have stayed.

"Cheyenne, tell me. You're killing me here. What is it?"

She slid off of him and stumbled toward the corner. It was a cradle. A wooden cradle, with two hearts carved on the head of it. She dropped to her knees, and her body shook as all the pain of eleven years and then some collapsed against her chest and concaved her heart. Colt was next to her in a heartbeat, wrapping his arms around her. "Darlin', it's not too late. We can still have a baby. Is that what you're worried about? That too much time has gone by? We're still young." His hands ran through her hair, and he kissed her shoulder. "Cheyenne, talk to me."

"You're going to hate me."

"No, darlin', I could never hate you."

"Yes, you will, Colt."

"Well, now, why don't you let me be the judge? But I'm telling you already, that's not possible. I could never hate you, Cheyenne. Never." He kissed the back of her head.

She took in a deep breath. He would hate her, but she had to tell him. It had been held from him for too long. It wasn't fair.

"We did have a baby." Chills ran along her arm.

"You had an abortion?" Colt released her from his arms.

"No, no, I could never do that. No. I didn't know if it was yours or not, and I gave her up for adoption. I found out right after ... Ron."

"We had a girl? I have a daughter?" He ran his hands through his hair and stood. He paced the attic floor in quick, fast steps, causing the floor to creak.

"Yes, it's the girl from the hospital. Jenn."

"The girl that needs the bone marrow transplant?" He reached down for his pants and slung them on with a fury.

Cheyenne's chest constricted into a tight ball. "Yes."

"How long did you know she was mine?"

"I just found out today. I had a DNA test done on Ron, and it was negative for both."

"What about me, am I a bone marrow match?" He

buttoned up his shirt. With each loop over the button, it was like he had closed another possibility of them. Cheyenne's heart stung. It was over. She knew it.

"No, you're not."

"Dammit. Shit. I need to see her."

"No, Colt, you can't. She doesn't know about you." She stood up and rushed toward him.

"What, you're the only one that gets to know her?"

"No, it's not like that. She doesn't know who I am. She can't. It's not fair to her parents."

"Her parents? I'm her father. What about me?" He ran his hand through his hair.

"Colt, I'm sorry. You have to respect their wishes." She reached for his arms. One last moment to touch him. To feel his skin. This was it. This was their final goodbye. Cheyenne had ruined what little chance they had. She had messed up eleven years ago, and the reality of her life crashed hard against her skin as Colt pulled away.

"Fine. Let me do that. Let me respect everyone and their wishes." He slammed his hat on and stormed down the attic stairs. Would she ever see him again?

CHAPTER TWENTY-ONE

Cheyenne drove the Escalade back to the place where Jamison should have been, but he wasn't there. She had taken off without him. Surely Colt wouldn't have left Jamison stranded, right? It didn't matter. Jamison didn't need her. No one needed her. Not even her flesh and blood needed her.

She passed the front of the house and went to the back by the barn. The straw crushed with each step. It was harsh and brown. Like the death of summer. The colors had faded away. The life had been removed. Like the sound of what could have been. It was too loud.

Her lungs were tight. Her air was being stomped out. Today had been too much. All her hopes had been silenced. Stripped away. Just like they had been all those years ago. Everything had changed back then. The idea that anything could be different now was a silly, childish dream that she should not have sought out. She knew better. Even with the knowledge, she couldn't help herself, not when it came to Colt, especially not after seeing him after all these years and knowing he still pulled against the strings of her heart the way he had back in high school. It had never been easy to forget him. The moment he asked her to dance at the

Broken Spoke untied a knot she had woven securely. It had been safe. Everything about her life had been safe up to that point.

Colt was anything but safe. He danced along the edge. Being with him was always going to be a plunge into an ocean of uncertainty. Nothing about love is certain. Cheyenne let her guard down to be with him completely. She wanted to have that honesty. She gave it, and he left it. He left her in the attic of her parents' old house, alone and naked. That was the end of them. Cheyenne opened her heart to him, and she ruined it with what she had kept all these years. She didn't blame him. It made sense. But this didn't take away the hurt. Or the loss of what she wanted so badly.

She swallowed the lump in the back of her throat. A ride would help her clear her thoughts and figure out the next step for Jenn. There had to be another way. She could play another concert in Tennessee. Get more people registered so she could find Jenn a match. If she had to play a concert in every single state, Cheyenne would do it.

With that thought, she pulled herself onto the white horse. It had been a while since she had ridden a horse on her own, but it was like being back on a bike. Once you've got it, then you just know what you're doing. That's what Colt had always said to her.

Cheyenne kicked her heels, and the horse took off into the field behind the house. It was all Colt's property. She would be safe out here away from any cameras. It would be the last time she would ride on his land. Tomorrow, they would leave and she could start on her Get Registered Tour. But today, she would ride.

Through the fields and trees, she let her mind roam again. Yes, she had wanted to make a go with Colt. Even though it seemed unlikely she had entertained the idea because she loved him. She had let herself slip into that precious daydream she'd had as a teenager. When she was so wrapped up in the fairytale of a happily ever after. But it was fantasy back then, and it was most definitely a fantasy now. Even if he hadn't hated her, it couldn't work. Their worlds didn't match up. How could they? He was a real-life cowboy with the cattle farm and whole life already set up. She was a Nashville country singer with a completely different setup. Nothing about them matched up. Nothing. She swallowed hard and let a tear escape from her lashes. Just one tear. The rest were gone, just like Colt.

The crackle of thunder sounded, and the horse bucked up. Cheyenne leaned into the horse. "Shhh ... it's an okay, girl. Just a little nature. Nothing to worry about."

As soon as she said that, lightning shot across the sky and rain gushed down. In an instant, Cheyenne was soaked. Okay. All right. This was the way it was meant to be. Cheyenne laughed. There was nothing else left to do. Her tears were gone. She might as well get in a few chuckles. It only made sense for the rain to pour down on her. The rest of the world had, might as well let Mother Nature have a go at it as well. "Go on, girl, hit me with your best shot," Cheyenne shouted.

The boom of the thunder was louder, and a shot of lightning hit a branch right above Cheyenne's head. The horse bucked backward, and the reins slipped from Cheyenne's hand. She fell to the side and her body banged against the mare in hard thuds, until her legs slid off the horse and Cheyenne hit the ground in a big crash.

CHAPTER TWENTY-TWO

Colt didn't know where he was going when he started driving. He just knew he had to get away from everything, from Cheyenne, from everyone. He needed to be alone, the way horses separate themselves from the herd when they are sick or wounded, to die alone.

Colt wasn't dying, he just felt like he was.

The sign was so bright, so colorful—*Texas Children's Hospital*. His daughter was in there. He had a daughter. Colt had a daughter. His chest tightened. He was someone's dad … or he could have been. They could have been a family. Colt would have worked night and day to provide a life for them. He would have been a good father, a good husband. He would have taken care of them.

But Cheyenne didn't let him. She took that away from him. She left, and then she gave away their daughter, *his* daughter. He could not get his head around it.

Even if she thought the baby was Ron's … What, did she think Colt would leave her because the baby belonged to someone else? Because maybe the baby wouldn't look like him or something? Did she think that little of him? She had no idea how much he loved her if she thought anything would have made him turn his back on her. Any child of hers was his too. How could she not know that? Sure, they were young then, but it was real. He would have manned up. They would have been a family, his wife and his daughter.

He didn't even know what his child looked like. Did she sing like Cheyenne? Was she good at math like him? Who was she? Was she loved? Did her mama and dad look after her?

Colt squeezed his eyes together, a scream forming in his throat, only stopped by the ringing of his phone. It had been ringing since he got to Houston, but he couldn't talk to her. The pain was too fresh, too raw. And the anger. It consumed him. He was angry at Ron for hurting Cheyenne, but most of all, he was angry with himself. He should have been there for Cheyenne, that night and when she left. He should have hunted her down and brought her back. He should have brought them both back.

"I can't talk to you right now."

"Colt, listen, is Cheyenne with you?" Jamison was on the other end of the line. There was an edge to his voice. Fear. Why?

"No. I left her at her parents' house."

"She came home. I still have her phone, and her purse is in the house, but she is gone. One of the horses is missing from the stable."

Terror shot through Colt.

"Colt? Are you there?"

"Yeah, yeah, I'm here." He forced himself to breathe. She could not have gotten far. If she wanted to get away, she would have taken the car. "Have you checked the ranch?" He prayed that she was waiting at Night Latch for him.

"She is not there or at your mom's. We can't find her."

"We?"

Jamison paused for a fraction of a second. "Case. I'm with your brother."

"I'm an hour away. I ..." Colt forced himself to

continue. "I need your help. Cheyenne used to always ride when she was upset. There is a trail behind the house. It leads to a cottage in the mountains. That's where she will be. I need you and Case to ride up and make sure she is okay. Call me as soon as you find her. I'm coming right now."

***

The drive home was a blur. He was sure he violated several traffic laws on the journey because he made it home in record time. He kept his phone on the dashboard waiting for Jamison to call back, but he never did.

Colt dialed Cheyenne's number. "Did you find her?" he demanded when Jamison picked up.

"No. We just got to the cottage. She's not here. There is no sign of her. It's raining pretty hard. I'm worried." His voice cracked.

Colt took in a sharp breath of air. He was scared too. Thunder split the sky and lit up the night. Seconds later, thunder roared. They would never find her on horseback. His ranch was too big. That's when he thought of the helicopter. He used it to locate his herd when they were grazing. That was the only way he was going to find her tonight. "You and Case stay at the cottage until the storm passes. The horses shouldn't be out in that. I will take the helicopter out. I'll find her."

"Hold on, your brother wants to talk to you."

"Colt. Don't. Don't take the helicopter. It's too dangerous to fly tonight."

"That's why I have to try. It is too dangerous to leave her out there alone." Colt's throat closed. He couldn't lose her, not again, not like this. He pulled back the doors of the garage and wheeled the helicopter out. It had been a few months since his last flight. The sky was dark other than the lightning that flashed above like an amateur war scene. He had seen these types of tunnel clouds before. Everything about his training said not to fly. He wiped his brow as the helicopter shook when Colt hit the start. His left hand squeezed on the collective as he pulled it up. Colt never flew at night, not because he couldn't. He could; he knew how, but flying to him was like riding a horse. It was only for work. There was nothing fun for him about flying. Tonight would be the pinnacle of this.

He eased on the left pedal. Once he was off the ground, he slowly moved the cyclic to move the rotor blades forward. He flew to the house on Parkside so he could follow the trail. Cheyenne would stick to the trail. Wouldn't she? Shit, why had she gone out at night? If she wanted to ride, he would've taken her.

The spotlight illuminated the ground. Ten minutes from the house, he spotted the horse. The saddle was empty. Colt's heart dropped. His lungs collapsed. No! No! She had to be okay. Cheyenne had to be okay. He needed her. He couldn't live without her, not now, knowing how it could be. They could make it work. They could get past this, past anything. He just needed her to be okay.

Colt continued to fly above the winding path to the cottage. She wasn't there. *Oh god, no.* Where could she be? He doubled back and traced the path again. The trail was steep, with sharp bends with a sheer cliff just before it reached the top. If she fell off … No, he would not think about it. He would find her. He had to.

Colt circled back to where he spotted the horse as lightning continued to light up the sky, crashes of thunder following only a few seconds later. Not much long after, he spotted one of his herds in the open meadow he had only just moved them to, and then he spotted Cheyenne lying on the ground, her red hair fanned out around her. Relief washed over him until he saw movement in the herd. The hairs on his arms and neck stood taught. There was frenetic energy radiating from the group of cattle. They were scared too, and scared cattle move, fast.

Stampede.

"Come on, darlin'. Hold on. I'm coming." He concentrated on getting the chopper in front of the herd. If he could drop in between them and Cheyenne, they would divert. But if he didn't ...

Colt lowered the collective. Almost there. And then he pitched up. "Come on, come on, come on." His altitude dropped, but his tail still had clearance. It wasn't going to hit the ground, but there was no guarantee the herd wouldn't hit him. Better they break the tail of the chopper than trample Cheyenne. "Come on, guys. Work with me. Change paths." Colt coaxed as he leveled out into a hover. The back hit the ground a second before the front hit with a thud hard enough to jar him in his seat. Not his best landing, but he was on the ground.

Cattle trampled past him close enough to touch through the left-side window. "Keep going," Colt prayed. *Hold your direction, keep going.* Cattle were notoriously fickle; they could change direction on a dime. Colt held his breath until the last animal had passed Cheyenne only five feet from her. If he hadn't been there ... He wouldn't let himself think that. He was there. She was okay.

Cheyenne sat up. Blood dripped from a gash on her head. Her shirt was soaked through, clinging to her body. Rain dripped from her face like tears. "Colt."

"Cheyenne."

"You're here."

"I'm here." Colt wrapped her in his arms, lifting her off the ground. "We need to get out of here. It's not safe. They could change direction. Can you walk?"

"Yeah. My head. I hit my head."

"I know, darlin'. You're going to be okay. Let's get you home."

Colt strapped Cheyenne into the seat next to him, covering her ears with the protective covers. He could not speak for the flight home. Adrenaline would not let him. His hands shook on the cyclic, meaning he had to correct for the small jerky movement. *She is safe. She is safe.* He repeated the words like a mantra, even after he landed back at the ranch, but his body refused to believe him. His heart refused to slow. He could have lost her again. No. never. He could never let that happen again.

"Don't ever go riding without me." Colt unfastened her and lifted her out of her seat. He cradled her against his chest and walked across the field to the house. "I mean it. Don't. I can't lose you. Not again."

He carried her across the threshold, where Jasper welcomed them at the door, tail wagging.

"I can walk."

"Darlin', I'm not putting you down until you're in my bed."

Upstairs, in the master bedroom, Cheyenne shivered violently, her body almost vibrating. She was too cold. He had to warm her up.

Stripping her off her clothes, he then carried her into the bathroom. This time she didn't protest, just laid her head against his chest.

Colt set her down beside the shower.

"Don't. Don't leave me." Her voice was paper-thin.

"Cheyenne, I'm not going anywhere."

He removed his clothes and they both stepped into the hot stream of water. Cheyenne wrapped her arms around his waist and held him as the water beat down against them. They stayed like that, holding each other, neither speaking until the water turned cold.

Colt wrapped a thick towel around her and led her to the room. He took the quilt from the bed and laid it in front of the fire. With a flick of a switch, the fire ignited. He lay down beside Cheyenne in front of the flames, their bodies still slick from the shower.

"Don't leave me, ever again. Don't … I can't …" The words caught in his throat as he held her face in his hands.

"I'm sorry. I'm so sorry, Colt. I was scared. I was so young and scared—"

Colt silenced her with a kiss. They would talk. They

needed to talk, but later. Now they needed each other.

His hands glided over her body. He needed to touch her, feel her … everywhere. She was safe. She was in his arms, and she was safe, and he was never letting go. "Don't leave me," he breathed against her mouth once again.

She didn't say anything, instead, she laced her fingers through his wet hair and brought his mouth closer. Her tongue found his, tentatively at first, and then with deep, needy strokes. Colt groaned into her mouth. He needed her—to live, to be happy, to breathe. He needed Cheyenne in his life. "Don't leave me," he said again. He would say it every day, beg even if it made her stay.

Cheyenne's eyes met his. The fear was gone. She was no longer holding onto her past. Their past. They could move forward now. He pulled her body in closer and eased inside of her. He needed to feel the connection that only they had. There was no one else when they were together. Nothing else mattered. The world quieted.

"Colt," she cried as he plummeted into her.

There was no holding back. He couldn't be slow; the need was too great. Colt rolled them over, his cock still buried deep inside her. He wanted her to ride him so he could watch her body move, see all the signs of desire written on her—the blush on her skin, the hardening of her nipples, and her face when she came. He loved to watch her come, even more than he liked to come. It gave him pleasure he could not even begin to explain. He would do anything to make her come. His body belonged to her.

Cheyenne rocked her hips against his, grinding her clit against the solid length of his shaft. Her mouth opened, and her tongue darted out, moistening her bottom lip. Her pupils were dilated, her eyes hooded. This was the face he loved, the one he would do all manner of things to see.

"Oh … Oh, Colt."

Colt held her hips and pulled her down hard; forcing her to take more, take all of him.

"Yes," she murmured.

He lifted her up and down at the same frantic pace of his thrust, meeting in the middle with a punishing force that made her cry out. Her inner walls tightened around his cock, like a code had opened a door to a world that they didn't know existed. He was the key to her locket. She was made for him. Only him.

Again and again, he pumped into her until he had wrung every ounce of pleasure from her body, and she collapsed against him, her breath hot in his ear.

"I love you," he whispered against her neck. "I love you, Cheyenne."

Her tears wet his face.

He rolled them onto their sides, still hard inside her. "What's wrong," he demanded. "Did I hurt you?"

She wiped her eyes with the back of her hand. "I'm sorry."

"Oh, darlin', so am I." He kissed another tear away as it slid down her cheek. "I should have been there for you."

"You didn't know. I was so scared."

"Of what? Of Ron, or that I wouldn't man up?" He wasn't sure he wanted to know the answer, but he needed to hear it.

She was quiet for a long time, but finally, she said, "I didn't know … who the father was. I thought it was Ron. I was scared it was. I couldn't ask you to raise his baby."

Colt shook his head and sighed. "You wouldn't have needed to ask me. I would have done it. Nothing would have stopped me from being there for you and our baby. She would have been ours no matter what. I just wish you would have trusted me to do the right thing."

Her face crumbled. "I was so scared," she sobbed.

"Oh, darlin'." He ran his hand over her hair.

She took several breaths before she was able to speak. "I tried. I loved her so much. I kept her until she was eleven weeks old. We were living in a tiny little studio apartment. I was determined to keep her and make it work. I loved her so, so much. I got a job at a coffee shop. I left her with my neighbor when I worked." Cheyenne sat up. The glow of the fire reflected in her irises. She held her breath before she continued. "I came home after a ten-hour shift. My neighbor was asleep. Jenn was in her crib. She hadn't been fed or changed all day. She was starving and had a diaper rash. I held her and cried. I couldn't do that to her. I loved her, I wanted her, but I couldn't raise her. It wasn't fair to her. She deserved so much more." Cheyenne wiped her eyes. "So I put her up for adoption. And then I cried. And I cried. And I cried some more."

"Oh, Cheyenne, I wish you would have told me." They could have made it work with the help of their families. Colt would have worked until he collapsed to provide for them, but he could not tell her that now. It would only be cruel. She hurt enough.

"No one knew. I didn't even tell my parents. I only told Jamison when I was drunk. I was so sad for such a long time. The only time I didn't think about her or you was when I was drinking. I would get blind drunk night after night just to forget. But Jamison saved me. He sobered me up, gave me an ultimatum, and told me to stop or he would leave. I couldn't let him leave. I had already lost you and my baby. He was all I had left."

Colt swallowed against the lump in his throat. Jamison was there for her. At least she had him. A sense of gratitude overwhelmed him. Colt wasn't there, but she wasn't alone. Thank God she had someone. Just the idea of her enduring that alone was enough to bring Colt to his knees. He would be eternally grateful to Jamison for being there for Cheyenne when he wasn't. Jamison protected her until she could find her way back to Colt.

Colt's phone rang, bringing him back to the present. He was tempted not to answer it, but it was Jamison calling from Cheyenne's phone. Colt had not called Jamison to tell him that Colt had found her. Jamison would want to know. He deserved to know. Colt got up and handed the phone to Cheyenne.

"Hey." Her face lit up when she heard Jamison's voice.

Colt listened to her end of the conversation, Cheyenne giving assurances that she was fine and then … "No, he is, J. He is. I promise."

Colt wondered what he had asked her, but he wouldn't ask. It was private. If she wanted to tell him, she would. Jamison was her best friend. It stung, but Colt needed to accept that.

Cheyenne cut the call and handed him back his phone, then pressed a kiss to his cheek. "I'm hungry, Cowboy. No point in rescuing me if you're going to let me starve." Cheyenne crossed to his closet and pulled out one of his T-shirts. It came just below the curve of her ass. "What are you smiling about?"

"My shirt. You're wearing my shirt now. I like it. That's the way it should be."

Cheyenne shook her head and laughed. "The last man's shirt I wore got ripped off my body. Lesson learned, Cowboy."

Colt pulled her in and kissed her. That's right; Colt was the man in her life now. His were the only shirts she would be wearing.

CHAPTER TWENTY-THREE

Case sat beside Cheyenne on the couch at Parkside. She didn't want to watch the segment alone, and she couldn't watch it with Colt or Jamison. They were too close to her, to the situation. Instead, Jamison was out running and Colt was in his barn shoeing a horse. They didn't want to watch either. They knew the story firsthand; they didn't need to see it on television too.

"You all right." Case squeezed her hand. "We don't have to do this. We can put on a video or go for a drive."

Cheyenne let out a breath. She had to face it sometime. Once it aired on the local news, it would be picked up. It would be everywhere in the morning. She needed to see what she was up against and hear the sound bites. Would Ron see it? She didn't care. She had spoken her truth. That is all that mattered. She didn't have to carry the burden of that secret anymore. That alone made everything worth it. He wouldn't be punished, but this was a small town. Everyone knew. He would have to live with that for the rest of his life. People would look at him and whisper and cross the street to avoid him. That was his punishment. That, and he would have to avoid every Clayburn brother like the plague. If Colt or any of his brothers saw him … it would not end well for Ron. That was enough for Cheyenne. It had to be.

But there was a large part of her that wished she had come forward before the statute of limitations had expired. She thought she wasn't strong enough for a trial, but she was. She had sold herself short. She could do it, or could have … had she just been brave enough to come forward.

"Maybe I should make some popcorn. Pretend it is a crappy Lifetime movie instead of my life."

"No matter what happens, Cheyenne, my brother loves you. I love you. My mama loves you. Every Clayburn in the county loves you, and we will stick by you."

Cheyenne gave Case a small smile. It was starting. Neither of them said a word during the segment. Cheyenne's heart pounded against her ribs like it was trying to break free. She waited for the smear campaign to start, to see what spin the journalist put on it, but it didn't happen. Cheyenne felt herself blink. The accusations that she had lied about the rape to cover for an affair had been cut, as had the footage of Colt and Jamison throwing Taylor Thomas off Colt's property.

Why the change of heart? Thomas was an ass. He was determined to deliver a salacious tale. He wouldn't let the truth get in the way of a good story. Suddenly, she realized why he had pulled his punch at the end. Thomas was scared. He didn't want to piss off Colt or Jamison. Having two massive brutes fighting her corner had its advantages. Cheyenne felt herself smile. The interview wasn't horrible, it actually wasn't bad at all. She could live with those sound bites following her.

When it ended, Case turned to her. "You did good, Cheyenne."

She shook her head. "I didn't. Your brother and Jamison just put the fear of God into him."

"That sounds about right. But it's over. You did it. You never have to answer those questions again." He rubbed her shoulder.

The knot in her stomach loosened. "You're right." The crushing weight that had been dragging her down lifted. She wasn't ashamed anymore. She never had anything to be ashamed about, but now she felt it. She stood up. "Let's go for a walk."

Case eyed her dubiously.

"I'm not scared anymore. Of Ron or Texas or my past. I want to walk down Main Street and get a sorbet or chat with Caroline at the post office."

"Caroline retired two years ago. She lives in Katy with her daughter."

"Well, I will chat to whoever works at the post office now. My point remains, I am free. Free, I tell you. It feels good." Cheyenne paused for a second. She could let it sit there or push the envelope. What the hell, life is short. "Sometimes secrets get on top of you and you make them out to be something bigger than they are. And then you start anticipating other people's reactions, and you let that determine your happiness." She stopped to allow Case time to process what her words meant. About him and his secret.

He stared at her, absolutely no flicker of an acknowledgment in his blue eyes. Either her allegorical musings were too subtle, or he played his emotions close to the vest like Colt. Either way, he was not going to confide in her. And that was okay too. As long as he knew she loved him no matter who he loved.

She leaned over and kissed his cheek. "Case Clayburn, you are a great friend and a great brother. Someday soon you will be a great boyfriend or husband. Whoever you end up with, I will love because I love you, and if they are good enough to earn your love, then they get my seal of approval."

He glanced down at the ground and then kissed her head. "You're a good woman, Cheyenne."

Case and Cheyenne walked down Main Street chatting to people as they passed them. If they had seen the segment on the news, they didn't mention it. Most people wanted to talk to Cheyenne about her music, but some wanted Case's medical advice, and not always for their pets.

"People trust vets more than doctors," he explained when no one was in earshot.

"I think it is just you. People trust *you*." She grabbed his bicep.

They sat on the rusted swings at the park and ate sorbet, talking and laughing about the old days while they watched the sunset. It felt so good to be able to talk about the past without any fear. She could remember the good things, and there were a lot, most of them involved Colt and his family.

The swing pushed forward and the sound of Case's phone interrupted the silence. Case stood and took the call by the slide, where he thought she would not be able to hear him, but she could. "Hey … Yeah … No, she must have left it at home … Yeah. Do you want to talk to her? … Um … Okay, sure."

Case returned. "It is Jamison. He is trying to get a hold of you."

Cheyenne suppressed a smile as she took the phone. Jamison had Case's number. Mmm-hmm, J got her seal of approval. "Hey. What's going on?"

"Have you seen Twitter?"

"Nope. Do I want to?"

"I think so. According to news reports, six women have come forward to accuse Ron of assault, three in Willis, two in Conroe, and one in Grangerland. The police are opening an investigation against him. You did it, Cheyenne. You gave these women a voice by coming forward. He is going to be brought to justice."

Cheyenne couldn't speak. She didn't know what to say. A strange sensation swept across her. At first she felt oddly relieved that she wasn't the only one, but then immediately she felt guilty for thinking that way. There were other victims out there. If she had come forward sooner, could she have stopped it? Wordlessly, she handed the phone back to Case. Emotions ricocheted from every hidden recess in her mind. She couldn't process how she felt. There was not a word for it, or maybe there were lots of words.

"Colt. I need to see Colt," she said.

Case nodded and dialed his brother's number. Silently Case and Cheyenne sat on the swings until Colt pulled up in his pickup.

"Do you want a ride back to your office," Colt asked his brother.

"No, I left my car on Parkside. I will just walk back. It is a nice night. Just take Cheyenne home." Case patted the hood of the truck.

Cheyenne waved goodbye. The ride back was quick and quiet. Neither spoke a word. Before she knew it, Colt was pulling through the gates on Night Latch. They had not spoken on the drive home. He was giving her space to think.

"Let's take a bath, Cowboy."

"Can you smell the horses on me?" Colt smiled.

"No, you smell good. I just want you to hold me in the bath."

Inside, Colt ran the water for them. Once full, he got in first, and then Cheyenne eased between his thighs. She sighed as she leaned back against his solid chest. His strong arms wrapped around her like a protective case. She was safe. Colt was her safe place now.

"Hard day?" he asked.

She thought about it for a moment. "I'm okay. I will be okay. All my secrets are out, and I have you. So I think I'm going to be all right."

Colt kissed the top of her head. "I think you'll be better than all right."

Words passed back and forth between them for an hour as they went through the last eleven years of their separate lives. The good, the bad, and the unfortunate. It was like a flash backward in each of their memories. The highlights and subtle softness of missed moments. When the water grew cold, Colt wrapped her in a towel and carried her to the bed. Cheyenne was embraced in his arms as the last memory flashed in her mind.

CHAPTER TWENTY-FOUR

Until We Meet Again

Until we meet again
Seventeen tears fell down my face
Never forgotten, you pretty as lace

Until we meet again
This is not the end
This is a silent pause

Too sweet to be true
Heaven must have spent a lifetime on you
Wish I could hold you tight

Dark black curls
Soft ruby lips
Prettiest girl I've ever met

Held you close
Kissed you once
Had to let you go

Until we meet again
This is not the end
This is a silent pause

Always in my heart
Will never forget
Wish we never did part

The idea of Colt and Jenn in the same room had only ever crossed Cheyenne's mind once. In a moment of what-ifs and hopes, she played the notion of going back to Cut and Shoot with Jenn just to see if Colt would be willing to give it a go. But Cheyenne couldn't bring herself to do it. She couldn't imagine how Colt would have reacted knowing about Ron if she told him. She'd been afraid of what he might do. If Colt were in prison, that wouldn't make Jenn and her life any better. And Cheyenne didn't want to live in the same town as Ron. He had said he would be back again. Ron told her it wouldn't be a one-time thing with them. Cheyenne shuddered at the thought.

Beyond everything nasty about Ron, there was a sliver of hurt that she pushed down. The part where Colt would be angry at her almost seemed worse. The idea of rejection had been too much for her to bear. Jenn didn't deserve that either. Too many families wanted a pretty baby, and Cheyenne had set out to find the right one. She had been part of every step of the adoption process and made sure that she would still have contact with Jenn on some level. Not as her mama, but just someone who got to see her and still loves her from afar. Cheyenne needed that. She had to have that. Without it, she wouldn't have been able to release her sweet baby girl from her arms. It was almost like going into labor all over again. They had been so connected. The way Jenn's soft brown eyes had stared up at her with that unspoken love. The kind of connection only a mother and child share. There was no getting past it. The day she let Jenn go hurt worse than any pain Cheyenne had ever experienced, childbirth included. It was like a hardcore wrecking on her soul. It crushed her.

That was the day she began to spiral. She drank to forget. It had been only a few weeks after Jenn was gone that Cheyenne got her first record contract. It should have been a moment of happiness for her. She should have danced all over Nashville, but instead, she downed a fifth of vodka. Straight. That was when she met Jamison, in a bar. Some other guy had tried to drag her drunk ass out of the place, and Jamison had stepped in. He had never left her side from that point on.

The elevator was formulaic with its dull exterior and the hum as they rose to the next floor. The bell rang. And Cheyenne reached for the wall to stabilize herself.

"Colt, she's sick."

"I know, darlin'." He pulled her body into his in the elevator. Cheyenne had called ahead and asked Maggie if it would be okay to bring Colt. She'd explained who he was and that there would be no mention of his real relationship with Jenn. He just wanted to see her. Maggie wholeheartily agreed. Cheyenne figured she would; they had always had a connection. Even before she gave Jenn to Maggie, there was something about her that made Cheyenne comfortable. Like they were family.

"You'll have to wear hair cover and gloves." Cheyenne stared up at Colt, his brown eyes soft and warm, so full of comfort. God, she wished Jenn could have gotten the chance to know him as her dad. *No. Don't go there.* Jenn had a good dad. Dennis showed up at all her dance lessons and took her for horseback rides. He had taught her how to fish and even sat down with her for tea parties. The man was a good father.

"Cheyenne, I'll put on whatever I need to. It's going to be okay. I promise." He kissed her head.

But it wasn't. Cheyenne knew this. Maggie had told her over the phone the doctors were not hopeful anymore. Her only hope was a bone marrow transplant, and no one was a match, not even Colt.

"I'm sorry I didn't tell you sooner. Colt, the doctors are not hopeful." She took a step back. She needed to be out of his embrace so he could take in what she had said.

He nodded, and the elevator doors opened. They made their way down the hall and into Jenn's room. Maggie's eyes were red. She was always so brave. Never showed a sign of sadness. This was not good.

The nurse handed Cheyenne and Colt the hair covering, mask, and gloves before they stood in front of Jenn. Her eyes were closed. A lump caught in the back of Cheyenne's throat. She glanced at the oxygen machine. The numbers moved. Jenn was asleep, that's all.

"Is it all right if we speak to her?" Cheyenne squeezed Maggie's hand.

"Sure, I'll let you have a moment." Maggie nodded hello to Colt and exited the room.

"Hey, baby girl. I brought someone here to meet you."

Jenn's body stirred, and she peeked one eye open. "You're back."

"That's right. And I brought—"

"Your boyfriend?" Jenn smiled at Colt. They had the same dark hair and warm brown eyes. How had she not seen it before? Jenn looked like Colt, but Cheyenne had been too scared to see it, to let herself hope.

Cheyenne smiled.

"That's right. I'm Colt, Cheyenne's man." His eyes twinkled with pride. His voice was like honey.

"He's cute." Jenn giggled.

"Hush now, you don't want him to take all the oxygen out of the room with his big head."

They laughed. The three of them, together. It was sweet and painful all mixed into the moment of a hospital bed and a dream that could never play out in reality. The idea of the three of them in a moment of happiness in sync pulled at Cheyenne's chest. Flashes of more memories like this, but not in a hospital. Instead at the dinner table, or maybe on

Jenn's first day of school. All that could have been, maybe all that should have been, was now gone. It wasn't meant to be.

"Baby girl, I brought my journal with me." Cheyenne peered around the room. The nurses had given them a moment. Jenn wasn't supposed to touch things from the outside, so Cheyenne found a pair of gloves in one of the drawers and handed them to Colt.

"Can you help her with these?"

"It'd be my honor." Colt gently picked up Jenn's hand and eased her fingers into the gloves. He was so tender with her, it tore at Cheyenne's heart. He would make such a good dad. Regret inched its way back into her mind. Dammit. She messed up. *Focus.* She could tend to those emotions later. Right now, she needed to be here for Jenn and give her everything she could in this moment. Be the happiness and hope for Jenn.

"Here, I've got some songs I wrote when I was a few years older than you. I thought that might be nice for us to sing together?" Cheyenne handed the journal to Jenn with it open to the songs she had written so many years ago. There were songs about flowers and a few about the summertime, one song about the rain and spring. All sweet songs were written by Cheyenne in her youth when she had viewed the world with a glossy-eyed, innocent outlook.

Jenn's eyes lit up, as if she had been given the best gift ever. An exclusive look at Cheyenne Ford's journal—all her secrets, thoughts, and songs no one else had heard or read. She flipped through the pages and skipped over the part that Cheyenne had marked for her to read.

Cheyenne took a step forward and paused. No, it was okay. If Jenn wanted to look, she could. Jenn stopped on a page and pulled the book in closer to her face. She read it quietly to herself, not a word was spoken.

"Did you find a good one?" Colt offered. His smile came through with his voice. It was so sweet, like honey. He was in love as he took in his daughter. There was no doubt. Even though she called someone else dad, it was obvious that she would always be his daughter in his heart.

"Yes, Cheyenne, will you sing this one to me?" Jenn turned the journal around and handed it to Cheyenne. Cheyenne's face heated, and for once, she was glad to have the mask and to be semi-hidden. She hadn't intended for Jenn to see this one. She had wanted to sing one of the songs she had written when she was in school, bring back a memory that maybe Jenn could identify with. Not this song. This song was not supposed to be seen or heard by anyone, even though it had been heard by someone many years ago. It was the song Cheyenne used to sing softly as she rocked Jenn. She swallowed hard and bit her tongue. She would have to sing it. There was no room for excuses. Cheyenne wouldn't tell Jenn no for any reason.

"Sure, sweetie. I'll sing this for you." Cheyenne batted her eyes as she focused on the floor for a second. She urged herself to be brave at this moment. Give Jenn this song. Do it. Be strong.

"Baby girl, until we meet again. Seventeen tears fell down my face. Never forgotten, you pretty as lace," Cheyenne sang the soft melody as she had ten years ago to this same pretty girl who lay in the hospital bed.

A tear formed in Jenn's eyes, and she nodded after Cheyenne sang the last word. Colt stood behind Cheyenne and squeezed her shoulders.

"Thank you. I think that's my favorite song." Jenn smiled and closed her eyes.

A sound of a voice came from the door entrance. "Visiting time is up," the nurse from earlier advised.

Cheyenne stood and turned toward Colt. He wrapped his arms around her and led her out of the room. Too much had transpired. Too much time. Too many emotions. Too much loss. Too many mistakes. The walls had closed in on Cheyenne, and she needed to breathe. They tossed their masks and gloves outside the room, and Maggie nodded at them. She made her way back into the room to sit at Jenn's side, and Cheyenne and Colt headed toward the elevator. They stepped into the metal box as the doors shut. It was as if all hope had been silenced. Nothing about Jenn's room had presented the idea of a future. It was all temporary. Less than an hour was their moment as what could ever be close enough to resemble a family, and Jenn didn't even know it.

Neither said a word or looked at each other on the ride back to Cut and Shoot. The silence was loud, and it spoke volumes of what was to be and what the future held. It hurt. Pain that couldn't be processed with a chat and a plan. This moment was nothing Cheyenne had ever imagined. It was so much more of the idea of loss. It's a different emotion. The kind where there is a small peak at something, and then it is ripped away. It's torture. A taste of something sweet and pure, but not being given the chance to ever really enjoy it. It had been witnessed in the hospital room. A slight glimpse of being a couple. Colt and Cheyenne together with their daughter. A child that had been made from love. Jenn would never get to experience being loved by Cheyenne and Colt together. The fruit of their love had been given to someone else. Another couple got to cherish their little girl. It was Cheyenne's fault. There was no way Colt would ever get past this. The deafening silence on their way home was a smack of that reality. His home. It was where Colt lived. Cheyenne didn't belong here. Maybe she did back then, but not now. It just wasn't meant to be.

Cheyenne got out of the truck just as her phone vibrated. It was Maggie. Cheyenne didn't want to answer. No. It wasn't to be this way. It couldn't be. It was too soon. The impending sound of doom blared against Cheyenne's ears. This is not how things are supposed to go. Jenn was only a child. A baby. She had just crossed into double digits. She had so much more life to experience, and for life to experience her and her sweet smile.

"Hello?"

"Cheyenne, they called just as y'all were driving away. I saw your truck through the hospital window. They found a donor. He's a match. Colt is a match. We just found out. He's a match. They ran the test twice."

"Oh, Maggie, I'm so … How? Why didn't they know before?"

"I don't know. I guess because there was such a backlog from before the concert, but he is a match." Her voice broke with emotion.

Relief washed over Cheyenne. Jenn was going to be okay. Her baby was going to be okay. Oh, thank God. "Wow, oh my gosh, what next? We can come back tonight. Will you tell Jenn that it's Colt?" Cheyenne asked hopefully. *Please let her say yes. Let us be part of her life. Just a small part. Please.*

There was a long silence on the other side of the phone, so long that Cheyenne thought the connection had been lost, but finally Maggie spoke, "Um … I don't think so. The bone marrow coordinator thinks it is best not to know … and Dennis and I have spoken about it. It's too much for her, for us as a family. We need some space to get through this. We are so grateful for everything you have done, but …"

Maggie kept talking, but Cheyenne didn't hear the words. She was being asked to give up her baby again. She closed her eyes to stop the steady stream of tears, but they found a way out and down her cheeks. Cheyenne had given Jenn up; she had no rights. Her baby did not belong to her anymore.

The dial tone rang in her ear. Cheyenne dropped the phone onto the dirt road and little fragments of it scattered over the gravel. It was shattered. Cheyenne fell to her knees.

Colt rushed to her side and pulled her into his arms. "No, tell me she didn't." He tipped Cheyenne's chin up to face him. His warm brown eyes were no longer soft and gentle. There was deep intense pain and anger that roared from his irises. "Tell me she's still alive."

Cheyenne nodded. "She's going to be okay. They found a match. It's you. You're the match." Cheyenne sobbed. Her tears were mixed with grief and happiness. She didn't know which one gushed out of her the hardest.

Colt dropped to the ground and grabbed at the pieces of Cheyenne's phone, little chunks of plastic and glass. He tried to jam them together, as if it were even possible. The phone was irreparable. It was broken and gone. Cheyenne sat on the ground. Numb. Colt lifted the final square and stood.

"I'm a match," Colt whispered. "I'm a match. Of course I'm a match; I'm her dad." Awe filled his deep voice as he acknowledged their bond. "When do I get to see her again? When do we do the transplant? I'm ready. Let's go back tonight."

Cheyenne shook her head. "You can go in the morning, but … you can't see her again. Dennis and Maggie don't think it is a good idea. They aren't going to tell Jenn."

Colt's eyes narrowed. "Why? I'm her dad. I need to be her dad, Cheyenne."

Cheyenne gasped for breath. The pressure in her chest made it hard to breathe. "No. You're not her dad. Dennis is her dad. He raised her."

Colt fidgeted with the phone as he smashed it together. His strength broke the phone into two. He gripped the larger chunks with the smaller pieces into a ball. "I'm her dad. The only reason Dennis is there with her now and not me is that you ran off."

"I know." Shame settled on Cheyenne. She had never considered Colt. "I messed up. I should have come back to you. I should have tried. I know—" She cried harder.

"No, you don't know. You don't get it. You have no idea. You gave up our baby. I didn't. I didn't choose not to be a dad. You chose that for me. You took her away from me."

"I'm sorry. You would've been a good dad. I'm sorry." Cheyenne grasped at his legs.

He took a step back, his eyes focused on the ground. "No. I can't do this, Cheyenne. I can't pretend that what you did is okay."

He backed further away. Colt turned around and paused, then glanced back at Cheyenne. His eyes were dark.

Cheyenne got to her feet. "Colt."

Colt turned on his heel and stormed off to his barn. She began to follow him. She needed him. They needed each other. They could weather through this. He said he loved her. Always and forever, that had been what he had said. They could try again to have a family together. A real one. Not just a glimpse of a stolen moment that was never really theirs to have. She had given that one away. It wasn't fair to any of them, but it had happened, and now Jenn belonged to another family.

"Colt." She called out to him as she made it into the barn. Colt was far gone. He had taken off on one of his horses and exited through the other side. He was gone. It was over. Colt didn't want to be with her anymore. It was obvious. And he shouldn't. She hurt him more than anyone could ever hurt another person. She gave away his child and his chance at being a dad. It was something she couldn't take back, and it was something she couldn't fix.

Everything she had thought was possible was just a small glimmer of a fairytale that wasn't meant to be. Her baby. Her man. It was gone, forever. Cheyenne fell to the ground and sobbed on the dirt road, and dust clumped to her cheeks. She shook on the floor of the barn until there was nothing left in her. Other than what she had before. Courage to get up and move. That's all she had left. It was what was built in her. A tiny bit of courage not to lay down and die. No. She couldn't stay here. She needed to get out of Cut and Shoot and as far away from Texas as possible. There was nothing left here anymore. The well was empty.

Jenn was going to be okay, that was all that mattered. That is why Cheyenne had come home. And now, she had no other reason to stay.

CHAPTER TWENTY-FIVE

Time to Go

Bye-bye, baby … it was just a dream
You and me a mere fantasy
I had my head in the clouds thinking it was a possibility
Time to go, the wheels are going up

No need to wave goodbye
You didn't see me leave
Best to take off on this runway
Escape this bittersweet melody

Bye-bye baby … it was just a dream
You and me a mere fantasy
I had my head in the clouds thinking it was a possibility
Time to go, the wheels are going up

It's over now
Every piece of me
No more lies, no more secrets
I've come clean

Bye-bye baby ... it was just a dream
You and me a mere fantasy
I had my head in the clouds thinking it was a possibility
Time to go, the wheels are going up

I told you everything
In the end, it didn't matter
Too much has passed
I couldn't be sadder

Bye-bye baby ... it was just a dream
You and me a mere fantasy
I had my head in the clouds thinking it was a possibility
Time to go, the wheels are going up

Colt couldn't breathe. No matter how hard he sucked in air, his lungs would not fill. His chest ached so much; it hurt so much. He didn't even know her, so why did it hurt? He hadn't lost anything he even knew he had.

Colt rode flat out. He needed to get away, anywhere. Just him and his horse. He couldn't be around anyone right now, not even Cheyenne. His thoughts raced. So many what-ifs. What if Colt had driven Cheyenne home that night? What if Cheyenne had come to him? What if he had followed Cheyenne to Nashville? They would have been a family. He would have had the woman he loved and his daughter. The realization of everything he had lost was like a lead ball fired into his chest.

The horse slowed when they reached the canal. What was he doing? He couldn't run. That is how he dealt with problems in the past; he would withdraw into himself and get as far away from everyone as possible. But he couldn't do that anymore. It wasn't just him. He had Cheyenne to think about. As much as this hurt him to give Jenn up, it wouldn't be a patch on what she was going through. Cheyenne carried her, nursed her, and loved her from afar for all these years. Colt needed to man up. He could hurt on his own time. His woman needed him now.

Colt let the horse drink from the canal, and then got back in the saddle. He dialed Cheyenne before he remembered her phone was broken.

When he got back to the ranch, there was no sign of her there, so he rode to the house on Parkside. The Escalade was parked out front, but Cheyenne's bags were gone. A lump formed in his throat. His gut clenched, and fear clawed at him. *Stop running, Cheyenne.* They both needed to learn that lesson. They weren't kids anymore. This was real. They both had to be all in.

Not knowing what else to do, Colt called Case. "Hey, it's me. Would you happen to have Jamison's number? I need to get a hold of Cheyenne."

There was a strangled silence from the other side of the phone. "Um … he is right here. We're … um—"

"Put him on," Colt cut his brother off.

"Hey," Jamison answered.

"Have you heard from Cheyenne? She isn't at the ranch or the house. Her bags are gone." Surely, she wouldn't leave without telling him, not again. Please, God, not again. Colt shook his head. This time she wouldn't get away. Wherever she went, he would find her and bring her back. She belonged here, by his side.

"She didn't tell you?"

"What, where is she?" Colt demanded.

"She's headed back to Nashville. She had to get out of here."

Colt sucked in a frantic breath. His head was spinning. She had taken off again.

"I'm sorry, man. I'm sorry," Jamison managed to sound sincere.

Colt's blood ran cold. "Is she flying to Houston? How is she getting home?"

"She chartered a private plane. There is a small airfield—"

"I know where it is. When is she leaving?" One

advantage of living in a town with a population under a thousand is that Colt knew everyone. If you wanted a flight out, you went to Cal Scott. Cheyenne knew that too. Their dads had been friends.

"Now. I think she already left. I'm sorry, man. I thought you guys could work it out."

No. It wasn't over. He would get her back.

Colt cut the call. He took off his hat and ran his hand through his hair. He could go home and get his truck before going to the airfield—that would take about thirty minutes. Or he could cut across the back of the Lewis farm and be at Cal's in twenty minutes. There was no choice to make.

"Come on, Leroy. Let's bring her home."

Colt spurred them forward and rode through the fields, over the fence that connected his land to the Lewis Ranch. His heart pounded against his ribs. On the horizon, he spotted Cal's Cessna. They hadn't taken off. Thank God.

CHAPTER TWENTY-SIX

Cheyenne wiped her eyes and pulled out her journal. There was no time like the present to write a new song. She scribbled out the notes that had played on repeat since the last image of Colt had crossed her mind. He was on his horse without as much as a goodbye. Just gone. He left her in the dirt. Soaked in her tears. Just like the day she had let Jenn go. All alone. Once again. This was her destiny. Cheyenne Ford might be country's darlin', but she was not a sweetheart. No, she was a brokenhearted woman never to be matched. This was her road she might as well accept it. Even Jamison had found someone. Finally. It was obvious in his voice over the phone that he was in love. And after such a short period. No matter, good for him. He deserved it. After years of being there for Cheyenne, he was finally going to have his chance at happiness in the arms of a man. Shoot, somebody ought to.

She dabbed a tissue under her eyes. Even though she shouldn't, Cheyenne reached for the flask she had stowed away in her purse. Pure vodka. That's what she needed right now. The burn of liquid down her throat. She would drown the lump if she had to. Cheyenne had done that before. It was something she was good at. Vodka made her numb. She did not want to feel. Nothing. All of it needed to go away. Not buried down into a place only to be brought up again. No, she wanted to erase all memories of everything she had experienced in Texas.

Cheyenne took a swig, and a wildfire of pain flowed down her throat.

It hurt. Bad. Her baby was gone. Jenn was going to be okay, but Cheyenne was losing her again all the same. To know she was out there in the world happy and loved was what Cheyenne had clung to in her darkest times, and she would cling to that now. Her baby was safe even if she belonged to someone else now. She was safe.

She didn't want to take her away from Maggie and Dennis and what they did for her. They were her parents. But she was Cheyenne's baby too. She let herself hope there would be enough room for her in Jenn's life. And she hoped that Colt could know her too, and love her as she did. *Oh, my baby.*

And Colt was gone; this time he had been the one that left her.

She was alone again.

Cheyenne wiped at her eyes. She was a big girl. She could handle this. She was going to go back to Nashville and hit the studio hard. She had enough material to work with over the past month to make at least one album, if not two. A tear trickled down her face. Cheyenne wiped that one away too. No. It was going to be okay. Or at least she was going to pretend it was until she got home. Then she would unleash the dam full of tears. A river of emotions was ready to break through and spill over her face, but Cheyenne was a performer, and she was not going to be a bucket of sadness for this flight. No, she would present the image of all is well. She had already arranged a car to pick her up from the airport. In a few short hours, she would be home. This was it for her and Texas. Too many sad memories and not enough good ones. Well, that wasn't entirely true. But all the good memories were overshadowed by the inevitable. The end of the storybook dream that was not meant to come to fruition.

Loss bye-bye, baby … it was just a dream
You and me a mere fantasy
I had my head in the clouds thinking it was a possibility
Time to go, the wheels are going up

Cheyenne put her pen down. Why weren't the wheels going up? She wasn't one to be picky, but she had an itch to get off the ground as fast as possible. Every second longer on Texas soil and the hot air was too much. It drained her. She needed to get out. Now.

Cheyenne unbuckled her seat belt and opened the cargo door. Usually, she was scared of flying, scared of dying actually, but today she wasn't. You couldn't get any more numb than dead. Not that she wanted to die, she just didn't want to hurt anymore.

She leaned her head out. "Hey, Cal."

"I'm sorry, Cheyenne, but the runway isn't clear for take-off."

"What's in the way?" Cheyenne glanced through the vast glass window. In the distance, a cowboy was on a horse. On the runway no less.

"Looks like somebody doesn't want you to leave."

Her breath caught in her throat. No. It couldn't be. He took off. Left her on the ground in a puddle of tears and pain. This isn't real. It must be like one of those images of water that people see when they are dehydrated in the desert. It was a mirage. Colt was always a mirage. An image of what she could never have. Something that she needed so badly but was only ever really in her mind. What they had was not anything that could last beyond the sip of tea on a hot summer night. The ice had melted, and the sun had set on them. It was over.

Cheyenne forced herself to blink. The cowboy was closer. No, stop. This isn't a movie. There is no way Colt was on a horse in direct line for her plane. This was silly. Cheyenne needed to sit back down and catch up on sleep and deal with the emotions that had rattled her brain enough to even ponder the possibility of Colt in front of her.

"Cal, I'm sorry to be a bother, but can you just get us up in the air? I can't be here anymore. I've got to go."

Cal laughed. "Cheyenne, honey, I might have been a daredevil back in the day, but riding into an oncoming horse is not something I'm willing to consider these days. Engine's going off. I'll be waiting inside the terminal." He tipped his hat and stepped out of the plane.

Great. Now what. Cheyenne went back to her seat. She was a patient woman on most days. She would just sit and wait for Cal's return. It wouldn't be long.

"Cheyenne Ford."

No. It wasn't him. Cheyenne shook her head and put on her earphones. Time to cue up some Lana Del Rey. If this wasn't a moment for "Cruel World," then she didn't know what was. Cheyenne sank back in her seat and closed her eyes. The soulful sounds of Lana came through her speakers.

"Cheyenne Ford. Cheyenne Ford."

No, not really. Just a mirage. Not real. Soon she would be above this Texas moment. There was a reason the state motto was Don't Mess with Texas, and Cheyenne was going to take it to heart. It was time to say bye to Texas for good. Fly high above the memories and missed opportunities. The what-ifs and heartbreaks. She would leave them all behind. Let them drift from her and drop down into the soil. Bury all of it here. *Come on, Cal. Let's go.*

"Cheyenne Ford. Woman, don't make me come in there."

No. No. It was time to go. *Deep breaths. Don't think about it. Just let it go. It's not real. Let it go and breathe.*

"Cheyenne." Colt's hands were gripped around her wrists.

No. Stop. Not real.

"Cheyenne." Colt took the headphones off her head. "Cheyenne, baby. You can't leave. You can't leave me."

"You left me." A tear escaped her lash. Dammit. She was going to wait until she got back to Nashville to let that flood roll out.

"I know, darlin'. I'm sorry. I just had to get away for a minute, and then I realized I was being an ass, and I rushed back but you were gone." He cupped her face. "You can't leave me, Cheyenne. I'm not going to let you go." He pulled a rope from his belt. "If I have to tie you up and attach you to my waist, that's what I'll do."

Cheyenne smiled through her tears. "I thought I was the one that got to tie you up."

"Now, darlin', we've got to take turns, and if my memory serves me right, I'm up in the saddle for this one." He wrapped the rope around her waist.

"Colt, you can't tie me up on an airplane." She tugged at the rope.

"Darlin', I just did."

He lifted her into his arms, stepped down the stairs, then placed her onto his horse.

"All my stuff. I can't leave my stuff."

"I'll have it delivered to our home." Colt hopped up onto the horse behind her.

"Our home?"

"Yes, darlin'. Our home. You're coming to live with me. I'm serious. I'm not letting you go. I know I've made a few mistakes, but I'm not going to let you leave my side ever again. We are both hurting a lot right now, but we can't run away from it. We both need to stop running. It hurts, and it is going to hurt for a long time, maybe forever, but we will be happy again. I promise you'll be happy again. I will make you happy."

"Colt, I … There is so much … I have things—"

"You are my woman, and I am going to take care of you. I will hold you when you cry, and I will pick you up when you fall, and I will chase you when you run. Eventually, you will stop running to anyone but me. I would get down on my knee, but since we're tethered at the waist, that would mean bringing you down on the ground with me. If that happened, well, I don't want to make Cal blush, as I can see him peeking through the windows now."

Cheyenne laughed.

"Cheyenne Ford, will you make me the happiest cowboy to have ever breathed the sweet Texas air and be my wife? Will you marry me, Cheyenne?" Colt dug into his pocket and pulled out a small leather pouch. He held out the ring for her to see. It was a sparkling blue topaz, just like Jenn's earrings.

A small fracture cut in the back of Cheyenne's throat, but she managed to stutter out a yes. Tears streamed down her face. "But you're going to have to ask me again on your knees at home."

"Oh, darlin', I'll ask you every day if that's what it takes to keep you. I just want to keep you forever." He breathed into her ear and kicked his heels. As if sensing a consummation needed to occur, Leroy sped off toward Night Latch Ranch ... which will forever be known as home, sweet home.

CHAPTER TWENTY-SEVEN

Play Me, Baby

You know the rhythm
The special one you sing
It sounds like an angel got its wings

The way your lips trail along my neck
It's soft and quick
Like a feather brushing up against my skin
Pluck my cords, baby, like it's a sin

It's a one-two beat
You've got me in deep
This is my heart; it's yours to keep
Swept me away ... make me weak

Play me, Baby
You know my song
The one that keeps me up all night long

I like the comb of your fingertips
The way you cruise down my lips

And follow through to my hips
Go on, Cowboy, give me that kiss

Hit that note
The melody is in the back of my throat
Your sweet words form my favorite quote
Your forever love keeps me afloat

Give it to me every time
Find the music on the line
Give me a B or even an A
It doesn't matter, we can do this all day

Play me, Baby
You know my song
The one that keeps me up all night long

Colt adjusted his tie again. He glanced at his mother in the front row, and then at his three brothers at his side. He was the first Clayburn brother to get married. No one would have put money on him being first. The barn had been transformed into a chapel. He could barely recognize the building. Hundreds of candles provided the only light. The hay had been cleared out and a temporary floor laid. Cheyenne's assistant, Katie, had outdone herself. At first, she scoffed at the idea of holding a wedding in a barn, but Cheyenne was insistent, explaining that the barn held special memories for her.

His mama smiled at him. He tried to smile back, but his face would not cooperate. Cheyenne was late. Colt swallowed hard. She was coming. Of course she was coming. Was she coming? Oh, God. He should have forced the issue when he proposed. They should have locked it in then and there, gone to a state that allowed same-day wedding licenses. He should be celebrating their four-month anniversary today, not worrying if his bride was going to show up. They had chosen to wait to make sure

Jenn was truly in remission. Well, Cheyenne decided, Colt capitulated, just happy that she had said yes.

Jenn was okay. Their daughter was happy and healthy and loved by them and by her other family. That is how Colt dealt with it, by seeing Maggie and Dennis as surrogates rather than replacements. His love wasn't diminished by them or by the distance. Jenn didn't need to know about him for Colt to love her. It was enough that he knew.

"Breathe," Case whispered in his ear.

"I will when she gets here." Cheyenne had lived with him since Colt took her off Cal's plane, but she had insisted on spending the night before the wedding with Jamison and her sister-in-law, Megan, and her assistant, Katie, at his house on Parkside. She thought it would be bad luck to see him before the wedding.

"You're going to pass out if you don't breathe."

"What do you know? You're not a real doctor." He gave his brother a sideways glance. His coiled muscles loosened a bit, joking with his brother always did that for him. Thank God, 'cause he needed to dial it back right now. Case was right, he might pass out.

The barn door opened, and Colt let out a breath. She was here. Finally. But it wasn't Cheyenne; it was Katie. She walked to the corner of the room where Cheyenne's band was providing ambient music. Katie whispered something in the bass player's ear. He nodded and started to strum. Colt's nostrils flared. They had heard the start of that song twice before. They were stalling. Colt's heart thumped against his ribs.

"If she doesn't show up, I will murder him," Colt said between clenched teeth. "Slowly. I will cut off one bit at a time. Any guess where I will start?"

Case swallowed hard. He still had not admitted he was in love with Jamison. It was obvious, but Colt pretended for his brother's sake. Case wasn't ready to tell anyone for whatever reason, so Colt played along. Not today though. Today Colt had precisely zero tolerance for anything involving Jamison Keyes.

"Call him right now and tell him he has precisely thirty seconds to get Cheyenne here before I hunt him down and tear off his balls."

"Tell him yourself." Case pointed to the door where Jamison was standing beside Cheyenne and her dad.

Colt took in a sharp breath. She was there. His heart jumped into his mouth. His bride was here, and she was beautiful. He knew she would be; she was Cheyenne—she was always going to look gorgeous. She could saunter down the aisle in flip-flops and one of his old T-shirts and she would still be the most beautiful bride in Texas. Cheyenne Ford was going to be his wife. His adolescent goal had been achieved.

The rest of the room faded away. All he could see was his bride. She was wearing an ivory gown with a corseted bust that fell off the shoulders, exposing her delicate peaches and cream skin. Her hair fell in loose red curls. Colt didn't have an opinion about anything regarding the wedding, but he had made one request, for her to wear her hair down, and she had.

The band started playing "Wild Horses" as she walked down the aisle.

"I thought you weren't coming," Colt whispered.

Cheyenne rolled her eyes. "Wild horse couldn't drag me away. It's like you're not even listening to the words, Cowboy."

He smiled down at her. His bride. His beautiful bride. Pride swelled in his chest.

The ceremony was a blur. He remembered saying "I do," and that was it. Beyond that there was nothing past Cheyenne. He couldn't even remember kissing her, much to his chagrin, kissing her was the best part of any day. But the ring was on her finger, and she had said the magic words in front of seventy-five of their closest friends and family.

A giant marquee had been set up beside the barn for the

reception, complete with chandeliers and parquet floors. Katie had agreed to the barn for the ceremony, but only if she got full reign with every other aspect of the wedding, so the reception was full-scale Hollywood glamour. A celebrity chef had even been flown out from Los Angeles.

The groomsmen and bridesmaids had already taken their seats at the top table. Guests were milling about looking for their spot. Katie had made sure each name was handwritten in blue calligraphy ink to match Cheyenne's eyes. He didn't want to go in. The only person he wanted to be with was at his side. Colt bent down and scooped Cheyenne into his arms.

Her eyes widened. "What are you doing?"

"I am making love to my wife." He took off toward their house.

"Colt Clayburn, put me down this instant."

"Okay, darlin', but our guests will get more of a show than they planned on 'cause I am going to be inside you in ninety seconds."

"Colt, put me down. We have guests."

"They will still be there when we are done. There is an open bar. Ain't nobody going anywhere."

Cheyenne wrinkled her nose. "Good thing I love you, Mr. Clayburn."

"It certainly is, Mrs. Clayburn. It makes what we're going to do right now so much better." He leaned down and kissed her before setting her on the bed.

"We're not going to have any wedding photos together if you take off my dress, because getting me into it the first time was a two-man job."

Colt was already pulling on the laces of her wedding gown. "I don't need any pictures. I will remember what you looked like for the rest of my life." Her breasts spilled out the top of the corset. He leaned over and sucked the dusk peak.

"Yep, it's not going back on." She sighed.

"Nope," he agreed without remorse. "You look

beautiful in your dress, but you look even better naked with me inside you."

Cheyenne laughed. "You are incorrigible."

"Mmm-hmm," Colt pulled her gown to the floor. Almost naked. "Too many layers. This is not convenient for quick sex. We might not be making it back to the reception, Mrs. Clayburn."

Cheyenne reached her hand behind her and unfastened her strapless bra. "Cowboy, we both know you can make sure we both leave here satisfied in fifteen minutes. Don't be modest."

"Fifteen minutes. So you're planning a cuddle after too." He laughed, then leaned down and kissed her.

Once her panties were off, he began on his clothes. His were far easier to cast off. "I have to ask. Did you have second thoughts? Is that why you were late?" His hands reached for her breasts, working the nipples into taut points.

She smiled and shook her head. "No cold feet for me, Cowboy."

Colt lowered his head between her legs. His tongue parted her red curls. Gingerly, he licked her, savoring her taste. His wife. She was his wife. She moaned his name. Suddenly, he remembered she had not answered his question. "Why were you late? I even thought you weren't coming."

Cheyenne groaned. "I love your voice, but you have far better uses for your tongue. Now, where were we?" Cheyenne laughed as she pushed his head down.

Colt returned to her clit, sucking and kissing.

"Such a better use of your tongue." She sighed.

Colt smiled against her pussy, then continued to lick her until her thighs jerked. He knew her body, exactly how many strokes it would take to make her come. And he would give her one less.

Cheyenne laced her fingers through his hair. Wantonly, she rubbed her hips against his mouth. He circled her hips and pushed them down into the mattress. "Why were you late, darlin',"" he asked her when her breath became shallow pants. She was about to come, but only if he let her.

"Colt, please," she pleaded as her head fell to one side. "Please."

"Darlin', no need to beg. I'm going to make you come, but first, tell me why you were late."

"Ahh," she groaned in exasperation. "You are using my body against me. I am not a fan of you right now."

"We both know that's not true." To prove his point, he lowered his head between her legs.

"Ahh, yes … Oh … Yeah, I am a fan of that. Please don't stop that."

Colt kept sucking, pushing her higher than before, but stopped just before the top and left her hovering in pleasure.

"It's a secret. I want to tell you on our honeymoon."

Colt sat up. "Fair enough. I look forward to making you come on our honeymoon." He winked at her as he grabbed his pants.

Cheyenne made an exasperated sound. "My dress wouldn't fit. Are you happy now? My daddy had to hold it together, and Jamison zipped. It was touch and go there for a minute. I thought I might be walking down the aisle in a petticoat."

"You were late for your wedding because you ordered the wrong size dress?"

Cheyenne smiled. "The dress fit me three months ago when I ordered it." Cheyenne took his hand and laid it on the gentle swell of her belly. "Unfortunately, your child has taken after you and is big and stubborn."

Colt pulled back his hand as if he had just grabbed onto barbwire. "You what now?"

Cheyenne laughed. "Cowboy, we are a cautionary tale. That's twice you have gotten me pregnant while I was on the pill. You are one virile man. Is anyone surprised by that though?"

Colt's mouth dropped open. "Wait. No, you're … No." He ran a hand through his hair.

The smile slipped from Cheyenne's face. "Are you okay?"

"My wife is going to have my baby! Cheyenne Ford is having my baby!" Colt shouted at the top of his lungs. His face hurt from smiling so much.

"Actually, it is Cheyenne Clayburn, but I won't be pedantic." She laughed.

"We're having a baby. Really? I'm going to be a dad?"

"Yep. You're going to be a dad. I am eleven weeks. I wanted to tell you after the wedding, just to make sure you were marrying me for my body and my incredible skills in bed."

"Rest assured, I married you for your body." Colt kissed the inside of her thigh, and then her belly. "And your mind and your heart and your soul." He kissed the sensitive hollow of her neck as he eased into her. "I love you, Cheyenne. Thank you for making me the happiest man on Earth."

"I love you too, Cowboy. Now, less talking. Make me the happiest woman on Earth. You have ten minutes.

The End

AUTHOR'S NOTE

Thank you for reading Cheyenne and Colt's story. I have always appreciated a second chance at love romance. For Cheyenne, she really needed to work through her trauma to be able to work her way back to Colt. In the end it was their love that made that possible through Jenn.

Thank you for reading and purchasing this book. If you enjoyed it, please consider leaving a review or recommending to a friend.

Thank you to Katie for all the brainstorming and support.

Thank you to Melissa Keir for believing in Cheyenne and Colt's story and helping it come to life.

Thank you to my editor Yezanira for diligently working with me to make this romance shine like the gold from one of Cheyenne's many CMAs.

Thank you to Emily's World by Design for her gorgeous cover design.

Thank you to my dearest friend Vanessa for our many conversations over the production of this book.

Thank you to my mom for endless chats and endearing love.

Thank you to my boys, for the happiness you bring me.

Thank you to Allen for your legalize, your protection, and southern inspiration.

GIA STONE

Here's a Sneak Peek at the Second Book in the Houston Heights Series...

Her Fake Blitz

Chapter One

This was going to be easy. Easier than her SATS, which Alex aced. She blew the hair from her face. A locker room interview. He was such an ass. But it didn't matter. Alex was having an exclusive pre-season interview with Cane Clayburn, the starting Quarterback for the Texans. He was coming back in after several rounds of surgery on his shoulder. Would he even know the difference if she asked him an off the record question? Probably not. The guy had idiot written on his face. From his blue eyes that held no thoughts behind them to the smile that was always plastered on his face. It was obvious that he had a simple mind.

Alex pushed through the door of the locker room. The man was a like a muscular machine and Alex held her own being an above average height for a woman. A good three inches above. She was proud of all five feet eight inches of herself. Even when she had stuck out in school pictures as a child, now she held her head up high. She had specifically chosen to wear her three-inch heels for today's interview. Given this, Cane Clayburn towered over her, even from the twenty feet distance. His head reached the top of the lockers. He could without a doubt touch the ceiling effortlessly. This was insignificant to Alex. She was there for a quote and to do a follow-up report from her first article on him and his shortcomings of last season.

He had his back turned to her. His muscular shoulders were bare other than a few drops of water that cascaded along them and the remainder of his back. A white towel hung low on his hips. Alex gasped.

Cane turned around and flashed a big smile, all whites. He probably had them bleached. He seemed like the kind of guy that thought highly of his appearance. "Huh. I thought you were a guy."

Alex pressed her lips together. "Nope, all lady parts over here." Typical. Of course, he assumed she was a man. He couldn't form a thought large enough to consider that the name Alex might belong to a woman or that a woman was a sports reporter. Internally her eyes rolled far back inside her head and jiggled around like a video arcade game that was trying to slam the ball in the hole.

In front of Cane, she brought out her smooth as honey side. The one that got the story. She was here to get a few soundbites and a quote that would no doubt be all over Monday morning's paper.

"You looked great out there today. How is your shoulder feeling?"

"Really good, you want to touch it for yourself?" Cane flexed his bicep into a large boulder of muscles and nodded at his own perfection. His eyes flickered at her like an invitation to enjoy his physical splendor.

"That's actually your bicep. Your shoulder is a little bit higher." She pointed to her own shoulder and demonstrated the exact spot of where his surgery would have been. Alex had done her research on the implications of a separated shoulder and what type of training and physical therapy would be needed for Cane to return to the field. Houston is a medical mecca for the world and Cane had received top treatment. His team's fate rested on those muscles and they were due for Super Bowl rings this year, if Cane's shoulder held up.

Cane laughed. "Ha, that's right I forgot for a second about your entertaining article. Though, next time you might want to do a better job with your back story."

Alex raised an eyebrow at him. Yes, her article had not exactly been full of flattery but there was nothing about it that wasn't thoroughly researched. Investigation was her forte.

"I'm glad you were entertained. Did someone have to read it to you? My articles aren't meant for an eighth-grade education."

"Funny enough, I was able to get through each one of your four syllable words. What were there three of them? Maybe add a bit more variety next time. You used the word arbitrary twice. Isn't that a writer faux pau?"

Alex bit her lip. Don't say anything more. Just ask your questions and get out of here. It was much too hot and it was not due to Cane and all his bare muscles. No, it was the anger that radiated through her. He was not going to get her goat. Absolutely not. She was a professional.

"Hmm...speaking of faux paus. I noticed you weren't quite able to get any balls in the end zone tonight. How are you feeling about the game next week?"

Cane's eyes dropped for a sliver of a second. If Alex wasn't a keen interviewer, she would have missed it.

"I'm feeling great about the game and about getting my balls to the end zone." He popped his knuckles. It was his sign. Alex had watched enough interviews with Cane to know when he got frustrated. He fiddled with his hands. Good. This was the moment to get the soundbites she needed.

"What's the back-up plan if you are unsuccessful? Will they pull you in the first quarter or let you try for five minutes of the second before subbing Bronson in?"

Cane laughed. "Sweetheart, I'll be playing the whole game."

Alex smiled. If it was one thing, she despised most it was being called sweetheart during an interview. It wasn't enough that so many players didn't give her the same respect they gave male reporters but calling her Sweetheart was her point of no return. It was time to stick the knife in deeper. She would need to catch him off guard to make him slip. Just like when he had his eyes on the tight end and didn't see the play from the outside linebacker. Like the one that took him out of the game last season.

Coming Soon...

ABOUT THE AUTHOR

Gia Stone is an author of steamy romances. Faulted characters, misguided motives, and misconnections are at the heart of her stories. She loves to collect passport stamps, savory memories, and race medals.

Gia's favorite quote is "The gem cannot be polished without friction, nor a person perfected without trials."